MURDER
IN SPACE

By
DAVID V. RE

I0541544

ARMCHAIR FICTION
PO Box 4369, Medford, Oregon   97501-0168

*For more information about Armchair Books and products, visit our
website at…*

www.armchairfiction.com

Or email us at…

armchairfiction@yahoo.com

DEATH STALKS THE ASTEROID BELT...

There was a place in the asteroid belt called the Hive. It was a deadly whirl of death filled with thousands of spiraling asteroids—where no spaceship could enter and return in one piece. And deep within it lurked an unsolved murder...

Terwilliger Ames was the best attorney this side of Earth; but when he was swayed by the charms of a beautiful young woman into accepting a murder case, he had no idea his life would soon be in grave danger, and that his adventures would lead him to the deepest part of the asteroid belt in search of a cold-blooded killer.

CAST OF CHARACTERS

TERWILLIGER AMES
He came to planet Mirabello to take it easy and do a little fishing. Little did he know he'd end up knee deep in a murder mystery.

BUCK WYLIE
One of the most successful orium miners in the asteroid belt— until he was accused of murdering his partner!

SUE WYLIE
Her brother was accused of murder. Did she make the right decision in hiring an out-of-work attorney to defend him?

MURCHISON
A hard-nosed newspaper publisher is one thing, but Murchison seemed to carry his role as a journalistic crusader a bit too far.

JUDGE AVERILL
His interpretation of space law could mean life or death for a man accused of first degree homicide.

FARLEY
He was the best attorney in all of Mirabello City—at least that's what everyone seemed to think.

SOUR TOM
This crusty old space dog was loyal to the end—even when his boss was accused of murder.

LOLA MORALES
She was the key witness for the defense in a murder trial, but would her testimony hold water in court?

CHAPTER ONE

IT WAS one of those afternoons with which the colonial planet Mirabello is so often blessed. Its twin golden suns blazed merrily from a sky of flawless blue, and little puffs of breezes chased each other through poplars and willows, and the tall grass at the edge of the stream where Terwilliger Ames sat fishing was cool and fresh. If there was a word for such an afternoon, it was lazy—and if there was a word for Ames, well that was lazy, too.

"Shucks," said Ames, mildly, discovering he had a bite on his line. He turned the massive book he had been reading face down, and, rolling over on his back, he gradually sat up, drew his legs up after him, and prepared to deal with the situation. He handled the bamboo pole expertly enough, though with little of the fiery enthusiasm native to fishermen, and after a few moments of play, he yanked up the line.

A fish came plunging out of the agitated water and swam in a wide arc in mid-air, then plopped down into the grass beside Ames where, thrashing about, it glared at him. Or so at least Ames thought as he regarded his strange catch. It was a small fish with blue scales that might have been made of some precious stone, to judge by their luster. Its eyes—they seemed overhung by angry, beetling brows—glared fiercely at Ames as it struggled, and its hooked lips kept opening and closing in an amazing way, until it seemed as if the fish was silently mumbling a string of curses at its catcher.

"Well, now," said Ames, "don't go blaming me. I was

just sitting here reading my book when you started up with my hook."

He reached out a hand to take the fish, when it began to change color. The blue paled to white, then the white became pink and the pink red, and the red very red indeed, and all this time the fish was swelling until it had blown itself up to three times its original size. It looked like something having an apoplectic stroke, and Ames, alarmed said, "But I didn't even have anything on my hook." And at this, as if his words had been the final insult, the fish exploded.

Ames jumped back and stared at the spot where the fish had lain. A little shower of hard, purple scales came floating down like the petals of a blossom, and there was nothing left of the fish but its lips, which were still cursing away as they hung from the hook.

He was still sitting there, perplexed, when a twelve-year old boy came running through the grass toward him, calling his name. "Mr. Ames! Oh, Mr. Ames!" the boy cried, running up to him. "There's a lady who wants you to be—" He stopped short and his eyes followed Ames' gaze. "Oh," he said, seeing the hook, "you caught a crazy-baiter, huh?"

"A what?"

"A crazy-baiter, Mr. Ames," said the boy. "Gee, Mr. Ames, you don't know anything about Mirabello, do you?"

"I'm afraid I don't know much, Willy," said Ames, getting up. "You mean you can tell from what's left that I caught a fish?" He kept looking at the hook, and he scratched his sandy head.

"Sure," said Willy. "They're little fish that get awful mad when you catch 'em, and they start turning colors like they were crazy, and then they explode and there's nothin' left but their lips—but that's the best part of it, because their lips are about the best kind of bait there is for other fish. That's why we call 'em crazy-baiters."

"Hmmm," said Ames, with a thoughtful grin. "Had me for a minute, I guess. You'd think that with all the trouble they went to, planting Earth trees and grass and flowers, and getting Earth birds and things, that somebody would have remembered to bring Earth fish too."

"Oh, there's plenty of them," said Willy, "only they usually wait for crazy-baiter lips before they bite. Seems to me you should know that, Mr. Ames—you've been goin' fishing every day for four months, ever since you came here. Didn't you never catch no fish before?"

TERWILLIGER AMES grinned again. "Guess not," he said. "I kind of lost interest after I left Indiana. Got too much to read these days." He picked up his book and marked the place. "Now what's that you started to tell me, Willy?" he said, gingerly removing the hook and throwing it, together with the lips, into the stream, where it sank from sight.

"There's a lady down at your office, Mr. Ames. She says she wants you to be her lawyer."

"Huh?" said Ames, startled. "Anybody put you up to this?"

"No, sir, Mr. Ames. It's the truth."

"Well, why didn't she go to Lawyer Farley?"

"I don't know, sir. All I know is she came into the office and asked for you. She asked me, 'Where is Mr. Terwilliger Ames, Attorney at Law?' and I said, 'Fishin'. Why?' and she said, 'I want him to be my lawyer. Can you get him?' And I s'posed I could."

"Hmmm," said Ames, thoughtfully. After a moment he

7

picked up his fishing pole, tucked his book under his arm, yanked a fresh grass stem which he chewed deliberately and said, "Well, Willy, I guess we'd better get back to town."

So down the dusty road they walked, leisurely, of course, because Ames wasn't a man built for hurrying. He was a tall, gangling sort of young man, with long arms and bony wrists and a big Adam's apple that bobbed around when he spoke, and from the way his face and arms were sunburned, you'd never have guessed he was a lawyer, because law is, after all, generally an indoors occupation.

A mile or so off, a bit in the valley, lay Mirabello City, with its population of 10,021. It was hardly a city, though it called itself that; but for that matter, neither was Mirabello a planet. It was really a planetoid, pushed far out into the system, a few days' jump from any of the larger system groups, but it was a very peaceful, prosperous place—peaceful, that is, when the miners weren't shooting each other, and prosperous when conditions were right. Conditions like the Hive, for instance.

For Mirabello City, like most of the towns on Mirabello, and there weren't a great many, was a mining city. It had its other industries too, like medicine farms and canneries and a bottling works—the Famous Mirabello Miracle Water—and cattle and dairy places, but mainly it was a mining place. It had been originally settled by miners who came to dig orium in the surrounding asteroid belt, and who had chosen beautiful Mirabello as their headquarters. And like most mining towns, it had remained more or less a frontier place, and therefore somewhat wild and woolly. And as long as the big ships came in for orium, and were Mirabello's blood stream, bringing in supplies, mail, news, even occasional settlers like Ames, just so long would

Mirabello remain a frontier, and all that that meant.

And now as Ames and Willy walked toward the town, Mirabello City seemed half-asleep in the heat of the warm afternoon. Not that there wasn't plenty of life in the center of town—Mirabello City was a busy place indeed—but the center wasn't the town. It reminded Ames of the town he had grown up in, in Indiana. Maybe that was why he liked it so much, and was so determined to make good in it and stay.

"Gee, Mr. Ames," said Willy, kicking a stone, "I'm just like you. I don't like work neither."

Ames grinned and said nothing, though he wondered how many adults shared Willy's opinion of him. Ames liked work as much as the next man, and better than some, but he was the kind of man such things didn't show on. And coming to this town hadn't been the easiest way to start a practice; Lawyer Farley and his friends had seen to that. If Ames had had his way, he'd have gone on fishing trips a good deal less...

WHEN they reached town, Ames gave his fishing pole to Willy to hold, though it fooled no one. Here and there he nodded self-consciously to people he knew, and he buttoned his shirt and straightened his tie, and wished he were wearing a coat. He might have sneaked in the back way if his client hadn't been waiting out front. She was sitting in Ames' big rocker on the porch, right under his Attorney at Law sign.

"Here he is, ma'am," said Willy. "He was fishin', just like I said."

Ames bowed politely and heard the words:

"I'm Miss Sue Wylie."

He held his book so that she could see its title,

MacDougal's Interplanetary Torts and Laws, and said he was pleased to make her acquaintance.

To tell the truth, Willy hadn't prepared him for her, though one could hardly have expected more from a young boy. Because Miss Sue Wylie was beautiful. She was a slender, ashen-haired girl, with a face and figure like those you get on good calendars. Ames took it in with one glance, and he took in more than that. When he met the direct gaze of her hazel eyes, he saw the trouble that lay in them, and for all the girl's good control, he knew that she was close to the breaking point.

"Mr. Ames," she said, quietly, "I want to retain you as attorney for my brother, Bruce Wylie, who has just been arrested on suspicion of murder. Will you take the case?"

"Yes," said Ames. "Of course I will. And now, if you'll sit down again, I'd like to hear some of the details."

It was a strange way for Ames to have spoken, for he didn't usually accept any kind of a case before he knew the details—that is, he hadn't done it when he practiced in Indiana and later in New York; but this was his first case in Mirabello. His answer had come out as directly as the girl's question. He nodded to Willy to leave, and waited.

Sue Wylie said, "I don't think there's anything I can tell you that hasn't already appeared in the *Twin-Sun*."

"The...the...ah...what?"

"The *Mirabello City Twin-Sun*," said the girl, a trifle puzzled. "The town newspaper."

"Ah, yes," Ames acknowledged. "You say the paper published the story this morning?"

"This afternoon."

"I haven't seen the afternoon edition," said Ames, mildly. "Is that a copy that you have with you?"

"Yes," she said. "They publish only one edition a day."

Ames took the paper without a word. The arrest had been given a sizable splash on the front page. The headline read: *Ex-Convict Arrested on Suspicion Of Murder.* Under that: *Buck Wylie, Notorious Gunfighter, Held in Connection With Mysterious Disappearance of Scotty Purdom.* A short, meager story followed. Scotty Purdom had disappeared several days before. An investigation by the Colonial Attorney for the Regency office had uncovered certain facts that warranted the arrest of Wylie. These facts were being kept secret until the indictment proceedings that afternoon, when the grand jury was meeting.

At the end of the article appeared a small note advising the reader to turn to the editorial page for further comment. Ames read the editorial. It was a plea for speedy justice and the refusal of bail in the event that Wylie was indicted. *"The past criminal record of Buck Wylie,"* it read, *"should convince the Court of the danger of allowing such a man liberty, especially since he can well afford forfeiting any bail and making his escape."*

"Nonsense," said Ames. "They can't refuse him bail." He had spoken half to himself, and now, addressing the girl, he said, "Tell me, Miss Wylie, is your brother a wealthy man?"

"He owns the Wylie Lode."

"The…uh…Wylie Lode," Ames repeated slowly. His face brightened and he said, "Of course. I knew the name was familiar. You see, I'm rather a stranger here; I've only been here four months. Perhaps you knew who this Scotty Purdom was, Miss Wylie?"

"I thought everyone knew that. Purdom owned the Silver Spoon Mine, the famous bonanza."

"I must have heard of it," Ames observed. "Now then, this business of your brother's criminal record—exactly what is that about?"

SHE hesitated. "I don't know much about it. I don't live with my brother. Six years ago he was convicted of killing a man in a gunfight over a mine in Tyuio. Gunfights were nothing unusual there. He was given six months in prison and a suspended sentence of five years. When he got out, he sold his interests and wandered around. Two years ago he came here and struck the Wylie Lode."

"I see," said Ames. "May I ask whether your brother knows you are retaining me as his attorney, Miss Wylie?"

"Not exactly, Mr. Ames. When my brother was arrested I went to him and told him I meant to fight this thing out at his side. He asked me to get a lawyer. I went to Mr. Farley. He said he didn't have the time to take this case. I think he didn't want it. So I came to you."

Ames said, gravely, "Thank you for your frankness. And now, if there are any other pertinent facts?"

"I don't think we have time," said the girl. "The indictment proceedings begin in half an hour."

Ames rose. "If you'll excuse me for a few moments," he said, and started to go inside. He paused at the threshold. "May I ask you, Miss Wylie—though you needn't answer—whether you believe your brother to be guilty?"

Sue Wylie said, "I don't know. I know neither the facts of the case nor the specific charges. And I think if I did know, I probably wouldn't tell you."

Ames nodded and went in. He changed to a dark blue suit and put on his new shoes. He knotted his tie several times before he gave up. If there had been more time, he would have fought the tie to the bitter end. As it was, he came out on the porch, blushing furiously, his law book and portfolio in his hand, and he said, "May I trouble you?"

She looked up at him, and for a moment her troubled eyes cleared, and Ames thought he liked the way she smiled. Talking to her, he had felt how badly he had messed up their initial contact. He had felt more than that; he had been unable to shake off the feeling that he had started something the end of which he could not foresee— something that left him uneasy. Now, momentarily, he felt better.

CHAPTER TWO

THERE was a large crowd around the courthouse, and the constabulary had its hands full keeping it in order. People sat on the steps and milled in the corridors, and many of them nodded politely to Sue Wylie. More of them stared at the gaunt, blue-clad man who strode beside her, his head towering above them, as if they couldn't quite place him. Once, someone said, "Why, that's Lawyer Ames! Didn't know him without his fishing pole!"

Possibly Ames didn't hear that. He had other things to think about. The suit he was wearing, for instance. He was the only man in Mirabello City that afternoon who wore woolens, he discovered, for when Mirabello wasn't working it wore tropical whites, it being a sort of tropical place to begin with. It wasn't quite Indiana, Ames was discovering. There were differences, small ones, but subtle, and they confused him. He wished he had spent more time studying the town instead of his law books. As for his books, right then he was probably wishing he had finished the one he held in his hand.

But he took his large steps calmly, and he was calm indeed when he sat in the courtroom, waiting for the prisoner to be brought in. He had introduced himself to the judge, a portly, good-humored man named Averill, and he had said something about wishing he had time enough to meet his client before the arraignment.

"Makes no difference to me, Mr. Ames," said Judge Averill. "I'll postpone it if you say so, but I can tell you all you need to know. Your client says he doesn't know a thing, and the C.A. hasn't opened his mouth about the evidence he means to bring out. So where are you?"

When they brought out Buck Wylie, Ames studied him casually. He was hardly any older than Ames, a big, well-built man with Sue's light eyes and her determined mouth, dressed simply enough in rough whites. He shook hands with Ames, and said, "I don't know what it's all about." Evidently, Ames thought, directness was a family trait.

Soon the Colonial Attorney, a harrowed-looking man of forty, got up and made a short speech to the grand jury. He asked them to pay attention and do their duty. Then he presented the facts of the case.

On the morning of the 10th, Scotty Purdom had put out in his craft for his mine. As was well known to everyone, the famous Silver Spoon mine was a mystery, as far as its location went, which Purdom had guarded well since he had discovered it ten years before. On this occasion, Purdom had borrowed an additional craft, because of unsettled asteroid conditions, and towed it with him, meaning to bring back a double load of orium, thus guarding his shipping contracts in case the weather subsequently turned bad.

He had been due back, the C.A. continued, eight days later, at the outside. He had not returned. His craft was equipped, naturally, with an AV and alarm signals, but no word had been received from him. Then, two days ago, on the 24th, Purdom's craft had been seen being towed by the craft that he had originally borrowed. Some hours later, Purdom's craft had been found in free space, empty and drifting, with a demolition mine bomb and time fuse in it. Purdom was still missing.

"The prosecution," said the C.A., "intends to show that Wylie was the man who lent Purdom a vessel; that Wylie later returned with his and Purdom's vessel; that the bomb found in Purdom's craft came from the Wylie mine. From inferences drawn from these facts, the prosecution intends asking this jury to indict Buck Wylie for murder."

Ames had been sitting and listening only too painfully aware of what he didn't know. But this was too much.

"OBJECTION!" he said, and he was startled at how loud his voice sounded. He rose, and with a puzzled frown, said, "Is the defense to understand that the prosecution is asking for a murder indictment on the basis of *inferences?* The prosecution has made no mention of the *corpus delicti.* How can a murder indictment possibly be granted without the preliminary introduction of a body? Unless the Honorable Colonial Attorney has made an oversight in his presentation, I ask the Court to dismiss the jury."

Ames looked around in the hush that followed his words and he saw that Judge Averill wasn't the only one who was staring at him. Even Sue Wylie had that peculiar look on her face. The jury seemed astonished; the C.A. let his mouth hang open.

Judge Averill cleared his throat noisily and rapped his gavel. "The Court declares a fifteen-minute recess," he said solemnly. Then, pointing a finger at Ames, he said, "May I see you in my chambers, Mr. Ames?"

So Terwilliger Ames followed the judge to his chambers. The judge kept looking at him for a few moments, offered Ames a cigar, and waited until Ames had lit both of them before he spoke.

"Mr. Ames," he said; "this is your first case in Mirabello, is it not? Yes, I thought so. Heard so, in fact. You haven't practiced much colonial law, have you, Mr. Ames? I thought so. What kind of law have you practiced, Mr. Ames?"

"Contract and corporation, sir."

"Where?"

"New York City, sir. Four years of it."

The judge nodded. "May I ask what made you come out here?"

"I wanted to be a lawyer again, sir, not a bookworm— that is, not a highly specialized bookworm. And I wanted to see a little of the system. I moved around for a year or so before I came to Mirabello, and I fell in love with the place." He let the silence continue for a moment before he said, "Is anything wrong, sir?"

"I think so," Judge Averill nodded. "I think so, Mr. Ames. A man's life may lie in your hands—yours to defend as ably as you can. I'm not sure that your ability warrants such a trust."

"But why, sir?"

"Because you don't know your law, Mr. Ames. Don't you know that Regencies outside the regular police areas of the I. P. have their own criminal codes? Don't you know that our code does not necessarily need the production of a dead body to indict and convict for murder? Think of it for a moment, Mr. Ames. We aren't living in an orderly, highly integrated community with a large police force. Murder is a simple crime when millions of miles of free space surround one. A murderer could dispose of a hundred bodies in space, or in anyone of a dozen convenient hiding places hidden in space. If we insisted on the *corpus delicti* in every instance, we might never convict anyone of murder. We might—"

"Excuse me, sir," said Ames, quietly. "You're perfectly right, of course. I knew better than that. I guess I was confused for a moment by the...ah...the..."

"The what?"

"The talk about the various craft and the necessity for borrowing other vessels because of unsettled conditions— the weather and that kind of thing. I just...it's all very new to me, you see."

"You mean you didn't understand what the C.A. was talking about when he summed up the case and explained about the loan of the craft?"

"Yes, sir. That's about it, I guess."

The judge shook his head. "That's terrible," he said. "You haven't the vaguest notion of what's going on. Do you want my advice, Mr. Ames—advice I intend giving your client? Give up the case."

Ames puffed furiously on his cigar a moment, then, laying it down, he said, "Thank you, sir. I have no intention of giving up the case. I've never given up a case before." He stood up and added, "I might also say that I've never lost a case before." He spoke very quietly, and he looked at his watch and said, "I've still some eight minutes left, sir. With your permission, I'll go back to my client."

Judge Averill nodded solemnly and watched him go out.

AMES went into one of the antechambers, where he found Buck and Sue Wylie. He sat down with them and said to Buck, "Before I say anything else, tell me one thing, Mr. Wylie—are you guilty?"

Buck Wylie looked at Ames curiously. "That's a hell of a question," he said.

"I know it is. What about the answer?"

"I'm innocent," said Buck. "Absolutely."

"All right," said Ames. "Judge Averill just advised me to give up this case. He's going to tell you the same thing, but I don't want to give it up. If you're innocent I'll clear you. Listen to me," he said, in dead earnest, "I've never lost a case in my life. I'm probably going to make more mistakes, but if you keep your confidence in me, I'll promise you that I'll win this one for you. I've got my own reasons for wanting this case. Will you let me stay on it?"

"Got a cigarette, Sue?" said Buck Wylie. He lit it deliberately, studying Ames' lean, earnest face. "Haven't run into many like you, Mr. Ames," he said, at length. "Guess I'll string along. For a while, anyhow. Don't know what else I can do."

"All right," said Ames. "Now explain that boat business to me. Tell me exactly what you know and what you did."

"Easy enough. About two weeks ago, a day or two before Scotty went out, I got a call from him. He wanted to see me. I was surprised, but I went to see him."

"Why were you surprised?"

"Why? Because I'd never been especially friendly with Scotty. Nobody ever had been, I guess—or don't you know that? Sure, he was a kind of a hermit, a miserly one at that. I hear he used to be all right until he struck the

Silver Spoon. After that he stuck to himself. He was always afraid someone was going to steal his mine from him—or that they'd follow him to it and stake a claim inside legal limits and share the orium with him.

"So it was odd, his wanting to see me, and it was even more odd when he said he wanted to borrow my boat for a big haul."

"Why was it so odd?" Ames asked.

"Because as far as I knew, Scotty had never asked anyone for a loan of a boat. He never seemed to give a damn about weather, and he never had worried much about keeping his shipping contracts on time. He pulled so much orium he didn't have to worry."

Ames hesitated, then said, "I'm afraid I don't understand this business of the weather and this boat borrowing. Would you mind explaining it to me?"

Buck looked at his sister, then back at Ames. "Where the hell have you been keeping yourself?" he asked, "Don't you know anything?"

Ames colored a little at this, but he didn't let it bother him. He just met Buck's eyes and waited, and after a moment Buck said, "I guess you don't know many miners, Mr. Ames. You see, some of the miners who work the asteroid belt have to pass through bad areas. Every now and then there'll be a blow—what you might call a sort of storm—"

"Vacuum impact?" asked Ames. "You mean that or spacial glides?"

"Impact, I think," said Buck. "Anyway, it means trouble. When those asteroids start acting up because the Hive's going crazy—"

"The Hive?" Ames asked doggedly.

"That's a big nest of them, close together, all sizes and

shapes and full of crazy motions. When they start acting up, you daren't get your ship anywhere near the whole belt. Sometimes that means a miner's got to stick close to his mine for days because the weather—we call it the weather—is so bad. Meanwhile the big cargo boats keep coming in here for their shipments, and if a miner's late with his shipment, he stands to lose considerably.

"So they pay close attention to the weather, and if it looks bad, they try to borrow an extra ship in advance so's they can get to their mines, load up fast, and bring both boats back before the blow sets in. The extra load gives them time, you see."

Ames said, "Does this happen often?"

BUCK WYLIE shook his head. "Couple of times a year, maybe, and generally most miners are stocked up well enough not to have to borrow a boat. So that was another funny thing, as I said, because Scotty used to pull out plenty on every trip."

"Did you ever lend anyone your boat before?" Ames asked.

"Sure," said Buck. "I've got four boats alternating all year, and my mine's way the hell out at the end of the belt, so the weather never bothers me. I've lent my boat out a dozen times. I've got all the money I can use in one lifetime, I guess."

Ames said, "So you lent your boat to Scotty?"

"And no questions asked," Buck nodded. "He told me where to meet him and I was there. Then I got back in his boat and he—"

An attendant poked his head in the door and called, "Recess is over, Mr. Ames. His Honor is coming in."

"I guess you'll hear the rest of it soon enough," said

Buck, as he went back to the courtroom with Ames.

They stood until Judge Averill was seated, then the judge motioned for Buck Wylie to come to the bench. A whispered conversation followed, at the end of which Buck returned to his chair. He didn't have to tell Ames what the judge had spoken to him about.

"After due consideration," said Judge Averill, "the Court has refused the plea of the defense to dismiss the jury. The prosecution will continue its presentation."

"Call the first witness," said the C.A. "Harvey Franshaw…"

Franshaw, a mild-mannered man of about fifty, took the stand. His evidence lasted less than a minute. He said he had been sitting in the Rocketeers Cafe, at the bar, when Scotty Purdom used the telephone. "The phone was right near the end of the bar, where I was," he testified. "I heard him speak to someone he called Buck. He said he wanted to see him the next morning, and Buck evidently agreed."

"Thank you, Mr. Franshaw," said the C.A. "Has the worthy counsel for defense any questions to ask the witness?"

"None," Ames said, quietly.

"The prosecution calls Timothy Saunders to the stand. Mr. Saunders, will you tell your story to the jury, please?"

Saunders carefully smoothed down his thinning hair. "Ain't much to tell," he said, grinning a bit foolishly. "I seen Buck Wylie with Scotty Purdom the morning of the tenth. They were talkin' together, standin' at the number three gate of the Standish blastport. A few minutes later, I seen both of them goin' off to where they had their boats on the field. Then they both blasted off, stayin' close together."

"When did you see them again, Mr. Saunders?" asked the C.A.

"Later that day. They came back, then Scotty had His boat fueled up, and after he'd brought his stuff aboard, he blasted off again, and Buck Wylie was in the other boat, goin' with him again. That's all."

"Thank you, Mr. Saunders. Has the estimable counsel for the defense any questions to ask the witness?"

"None."

"The prosecution calls Harry Reichard to the stand. Mr. Reichard, where were you on the afternoon of the twenty-fourth, two days ago?"

"I was out in my boat, hovering around the Grey Mountain area, checking a valve leak that had been giving me trouble."

"What made you go to so lonely a place, Mr. Reichard?"

"The valve leak, as I was saying. I didn't want any other craft around me because I was testing my boat, and I got some speed out of her every now and then."

"Did you see anything unusual, Mr. Reichard?"

"Yes and no, Mr. Whitley. I mean I didn't think it was unusual when I saw it, but later on it turned out to be unusual." He held a hand up to the C.A. "Hold on, I'm getting to it," he said. "What I saw was Buck Wylie's boat, the one that's known as the *Hellcat*, towing Scotty Purdom's boat."

"In what direction were these two vessels traveling?"

"South by east, land compass. That would be about 3 point 7. I didn't think anything of it then because Buck Wylie has his own blastport down that way."

"Mr. Reichard, did anything unusual happen at that time?"

"Yes and no, Mr. Whitley—that is, I didn't think so

then. I stuck out my signal flag and gave them a friendly hello. I didn't get any answer, though they couldn't have missed my signal. I thought maybe they were in some kind of trouble, but when I started coming closer, the first boat just opened the throttle and roared away. I figured maybe Buck Wylie was having one of his black days and let it go at that."

"Thank you, Mr. Reichard. Has the learned counsel for the defense any questions to ask this witness?"

"Just one," said Ames. He half rose from his chair, crouching over, as if his question didn't warrant getting up. "Mr. Reichard, did you see either of the Occupants in either of the boats?"

"No, sir. I was too far off, but when I started getting up—"

"Thank you," Ames interrupted, sitting down.

COLONIAL ATTORNEY WHITLEY was facing the small audience that had been permitted into the courtroom. He looked toward a heavy, florid-faced man whose grave, important manner distinguished him from the small group in which he sat, and he shrugged and smiled. The gesture was meant as much for the jury as for the man. It implied that the C.A. neither understood nor was concerned with anything Ames said or did.

Ames leaned over to Buck Wylie. "Who's that man there?" he said.

"John Murchison," said Wylie. "He's the publisher of the town newspaper, the *Twin-Sun*."

"Could have guessed as much," said Ames, turning back to the C.A.

Whitley said, dryly, "If my honored colleague is through conferring, I will call Robert Halloway as witness for the prosecution."

An old, white-haired man, dressed in miner's clothes, walked slowly to the stand. The judge and he exchanged nods, and the C.A. said, "Bob, suppose you tell us what happened to you the afternoon—"

" 'Twas evening," the old man said, crisply. "Almost night."

"...the evening of the twenty-fourth," Whitley finished.

The old man stretched his legs and settled back in the chair. "I was just comin' in from my diggin's. Been away 'bout three weeks, so I didn't know Scotty'd gone out and was overdue. I was sailin' along at four thousand, gettin' ready to pick up the Standish beam for a landin', when I saw Scotty Purdom's boat. I didn't know whose boat it was then, and I didn't care, because I'd almost run smack into it.

"The damn boat was idlin' along at my level, goin' in a small circle, without no runnin' lights, no signals or nothin'. If my alarm hadn't popped off, I'd have been sheared in half by her. Well, sir, I let out a howl they heard in Standish—I'd just opened my AV to tell 'em I was comin'—and I cut over and came up alongside. I tried to contact her on the AV, but she didn't answer. She just kept goin' round and round in a quarter-mile circle over the ridge near Gray Mountain, and not a sign of life in her anywhere.

"So I heaved to and drew up closer, till I contacted her. With the grapplers, I mean. I tied up fast to her and burned her lock open with a torch and went in, lettin' her carry my boat with her. And the first thing I saw—right smack in the middle of the main deck, near the control board—was a big five hundred pound son-of-a-gun demolition bomb, and a time fuse attached to her, blazin' away.

"Well, sir, I was about half a minute from goin' to my eternal reward. I just flattened out and dived on that fuse and put it out with my bare hands, gettin' a fine burn for it."

He held up his palms. They were covered with ugly, seared blisters that reached along the inside of his hands to his wrists.

"Don't want no bandages," he explained, half defiantly. "Sun's the best healer there is. You let the sun get at you and you'll live—"

"What about the boat, Bob?" Judge Averill said, tolerantly.

"Yep, the boat. Well, I put the fuse out and disconnected the bomb. I tried to call Standish port, but the AV had been put out of commission. I went through the boat, and there wasn't a soul on her. Then I looked at the bomb. The fuse'd been goin' about ten minutes; and the bomb had Buck Wylie's seal and registry number on her. Then I went back to my boat and called Standish and came on in. They wanted me to detach Scotty's boat, but I wouldn't hear of it. Made the best landing—"

"Thank you, Bob," said Whitley.

"Has the—"

"None," said Ames, dryly.

The C.A. turned to the jury with the air of a man whose job had been too simple. "Mr. Wylie," he said, politely, "may I prevail upon you to answer a few questions?"

Ames pulled Buck back to his chair. "The defense requests that all questions to Mr. Wylie be submitted in writing," he said.

"Really, Mr. Ames," Whitley objected, "this is not a trial—"

"As I am well aware," Ames drawled, "though it has been conducted as such. Evidently the prosecution has gathered more than enough evidence to prove its indictment. That it has presented such evidence seems to me to indicate an attempt to force my client to defend himself prematurely—in other words, to indicate his line of defense—"

"Objection!" Whitley cried. "I object to this innuendo!"

"Mr. Ames," said Judge Averill, surprise in his voice, "do I understand you to say that you agree with the indictment of your client?"

AMES hesitated briefly before he spoke. From the corner of his eye he glanced at Sue Wylie, and he saw that her brother had not missed that sidewise glance, "Yes, sir," Ames said, quietly. "I believe the prosecution can present enough evidence to warrant an indictment."

It was like dropping a bomb into the room. Ames flushed and seemed to shrivel under the eyes that looked at him. He sat down and met the astonished gaze of Buck Wylie, and he started to say something and changed his mind and was silent. He turned to regard the C.A., who had been completely taken by surprise by Ames' statement.

Slowly, the C.A. regained his composure. He faced the jury, threw his hands up helplessly and said, "That's it, gentlemen. The prosecution stands by the words of the counsel for defense."

Judge Averill rose to declare a recess, but the jury foreman, who had taken a quick look around the panel, said, "Your Honor, we don't need any more time. We're ready to bring in—"

The Judge brought his gavel down sharply. "You'll take the time!" he said, snorting. "May I remind this jury that it is their duty to return a verdict based *solely* upon the evidence presented, and not upon its evaluation by either the prosecution or defense. In fewer words, the prosecution's claim that its evidence is good enough does not make it so. Neither does such a statement from the defense have any validity in this matter." He paused, looking at Ames, and added, "I might point out that counsel for defense merely stated he believed enough evidence *could* be presented—not that it *had* been presented. The decision rests with you, gentlemen. Recess."

As the jury started filing out, Buck Wylie grabbed Ames' arm. "What the hell are you doing?" he demanded, fiercely. "He hadn't shown a thing yet. He didn't have anything on me!"

Ames said, "What would you have answered if he'd asked you where you were during—" He broke off. "Excuse me. The judge wants me."

Ames walked up to the judge, who had motioned to Ames from the door to his chambers. "Mr. Ames," he said, closing the door, "may I ask what motive you had for your strange statement regarding the evidence?"

"I'm sorry. I'd rather not answer that."

"I see," said Averill, thoughtfully. "You are aware that it is the duty of the Court to protect a defendant even though he may be represented by counsel?"

"If counsel is incompetent, yes, sir."

"I must ask you to bring your credentials to me, Mr. Ames."

"Yes, sir. May I ask when?"

"I'll give you twenty-four hours, Mr. Ames."

An attendant knocked. "The jury's back, Your Honor," he said.

As Ames sat down beside Buck Wylie again, he noticed how drawn Wylie was. "Relax," he said, quietly. "You'll be indicted, all right. I'm saving my guns for the fight for bail."

Sue Wylie asked, anxiously, "You think they'll refuse bail?"

"Not if I can help it," said Ames.

The foreman of the jury had risen. He handed a sealed envelope to a clerk, who opened and read it. "The grand jury hereby indicts Buck Wylie for the murder of Scotty Purdom."

Judge Averill rapped for silence and instructed the clerk to enter the verdict. He called Buck before the bench. Ames stood up with him and said, "May I petition the Court to release my client in bail sufficient to maintain security?"

Whitley was up like a flash. "I ask that the defendant be denied bail, Your Honor…" he cried. He opened a folder and flourished a newspaper clipping. "In connection with this request for bail, may I read this editorial from the *Twin-Sun* which—

"Objection," said Ames. "The opinions of a newspaper have no bearing on my client's legal claim to liberty before he has been found guilty. May I cite the case of Worth vs. Worth, Northwest proceedings, Volume 122? I object, moreover, to the introduction of hearsay evidence intended to harm the reputation of my client. In this connection, may I cite the case of Mars Trading Corp. vs. Jackson, Mars Superior Court, Volumes 34 and 3S?"

Colonial Attorney Whitley stood amazed by Ames' speech. He took a deep breath, snapped, "Not at all!" and crossed quickly to the rail. After a hurried consultation with Murchison, Whitley took a briefcase from Murchison and opened it. He took out a sheaf of papers, which he brought to Judge Averill's bench.

"Your Honor, I submit here certified evidence of the defendant's criminal record, and point out that his wealth makes any bail a mere pawn in his struggle for freedom. I further point out—"

"Objection," said Ames, raising his voice slightly. "May I point out to the Court the abnormal interest taken in these proceedings by the editor of the *Mirabello Twin-Sun*? I charge him with attempting to influence this Court, and maintain that his editorial is grounds for an action holding him in contempt of Court."

Judge Averill waited a moment before he spoke. "Objection over-ruled," he said, very quietly. "Mr. Ames, this Court is quite capable of arriving at decisions without the aid of newspapers." He studied the papers carefully. Presently he looked up. "In view of the defendant's previous conviction, and after consideration of his present ability to forfeit any bail this Court may set, and after consideration of the nature of the indictment herein returned, this Court grants the petition of the prosecution. Bail denied."

"But that's impossible!" Ames exclaimed. "That's penalizing a man for being wealthy, as well as persecuting him for a previous crime! In the case of Trotter vs. the Appellate Division of—"

"Mr. Ames, another word and I will hold you in contempt of Court!"

Ames stood there, his fists clenched.

Watching the armed guards escort Buck Wylie from the courtroom, he thought, for no especial reason, of the fish he had caught that afternoon. This had been another fish. He had caught it, only to have it explode in his face...

CHAPTER THREE

AMES watched the girl crying quietly. He wished he was more useful in a situation like this. He was helpless before a crying woman, and this time, maybe because the woman was so beautiful, and because at least part of the reason for her crying lay with him, he felt especially helpless. But it was more than that. He didn't really understand what had happened.

He had foreseen most of it, he thought, right up to the end. He had been certain he would have Buck out on bail. Perhaps then he would have had a chance at getting to the bottom of things. Right now they were pretty hopelessly confused.

He touched the girl's shoulder again. They were the only ones left in the courtroom. "Please," he said, "there's no reason to cry. Nothing's happened yet. I was sure he'd be indicted—"

She looked up then, and her eyes were strangely dry. "Why?" she asked. "You didn't fight for him. You let them indict him."

"I had to," said Ames. "It was either that or they'd have convicted him here without a trial. If I'd let them make the points they wanted to make, he'd never have been able to look forward to a fair trial. That publisher Murchison would have had all the ammunition he wanted. I don't know what he's up to, or why he's so hellishly bent on seeing your brother in jail, but I'll get to the bottom of it."

"No," said the girl, slowly. "It's impossible. We can't

let you be Buck's attorney. You'll kill him. It isn't your fault, but you'll kill him if we let you."

"What?" said Ames, bewildered. "I don't understand."

"That's it," the girl said. "There's too much you don't understand. I didn't know why you angered Judge Averill so much by implying that Murchison was doing something wrong. Now I see it was because you didn't know."

"Didn't know what?"

"That Murchison was Scotty Purdom's only friend. That he was a partner in Scotty's mine. That his interest in this case was the most natural thing in the world." She stood up and picked up her bag. "I see you're astonished again," she said, quietly. "Well, that's the way it is. Murchison only wanted justice, but now you've made him an enemy who won't stop at justice alone."

She started walking out and Ames, grabbing his book and briefcase, followed her. "What are you going to do?" he asked her.

"I'm going to try to see my brother now and make other plans."

"I can't let you do that," said Ames.

"I'm afraid you've no choice. I'll pay your fee, whatever it is."

They were on the courthouse steps now, and the curious crowds were looking at them. Ames walked along beside the girl, conscious of the stares. "Hey, Mr. Ames!" someone called, "tell us what happened in the case of Ames vs. Whitley, Volume I!" There was a roar of laughter at this. Ames flushed, realizing that the account of the indictment was spreading through the town. He had a long way to go, and the road was far from clear.

Sue Wylie turned off at the next corner, and seeing Ames still beside her, she stopped.

"I'm going with you," Ames said, doggedly. "I've got to show you that I'm the lawyer for you, and please..." he said, heading her answer off, "...do me just one favor. Don't express any opinion to your brother until I've talked to him. Pretend you still have faith in me until then."

She looked up into Ames' clear eyes.

Ames said, quietly, "Please. Trust me."

"I'll go with you," said Sue.

THEY hardly spoke during the ten minutes it took them to reach the Jail and be ushered into Buck Wylie's cell. When Ames went in, he saw that Buck's face was as dark as a thundercloud. He looked from his sister to Ames and said nothing, waiting.

"We've only ten minutes," Ames said, sitting down with Sue, "so we'll have to be quick. Believe me, I know everything that's going on in your mind, but there are reasons for what I did."

"For instance?" said Buck, staring at the floor.

"You wanted to take the stand," said Ames. "I stopped you because you would have been asked questions you couldn't answer. Suppose Whitley had asked you where you were for a few days previous to the time that the old man said he saw your ship towing Purdom's—what would you have said?"

After a momentary silence, Buck looked up quickly. "I'd have told the truth," he said. "I was out on a prospecting trip."

"Alone?"

"Yes."

"How long were you gone?"

"Five—no, six days."

Ames nodded. "Well, there's one answer. You have no

alibi."

"I don't get what you're driving at."

"I think you do," said Ames. "Whoever was in your boat two days ago, towing Scotty's boat behind it so that Bob Halloway could see it—whoever was in it knew two things: first, that you were going away on a lone trip; second, that you were due back that day. Suppose you told the jury that during the time someone followed Scotty to his secret mine, killed him, then brought his boat back— that during that time you were on a lone prospecting trip? Row much water would that story carry?"

"I don't give a damn how much water it would carry!" Buck said. "I was out prospecting. Everybody knows I go out regularly the third week in the month."

"Hmmmm," said Ames. "If *everybody* knows it, that complicates matters. But you could theoretically have gone to Scotty's mine in that time, killed him, and then brought his boat back."

"Why should I bring his boat back?"

"Because you were afraid to leave it at the mine. Or maybe you wanted to blow it up, have the explosion heard, have the wreck found, and establish Scotty's death as an accident right here on Mirabello."

Buck sat quietly a few moments. "It's a good theory," he admitted, at length. "But if I wanted to make it an accident, I'd have had Scotty's body aboard, so it would look as if he'd been killed in it."

"Hardly necessary," said Ames. "An explosion of a five hundred pound bomb could be assumed to have destroyed the last vestige of Scotty Purdom, especially if it had taken place over a wild, mountainous terrain as Grey Mountain seems to be." He nodded, adding, "Still, the fact that the murderer didn't include Scotty's body aboard a ship he was certain would be exploded inclines me to think he couldn't take Scotty's body back with him. Otherwise he might even have undertaken that slight detail."

Again Buck was silent.

Ames said, "You didn't run across anyone while you were on your trip? Anybody who might be a witness for you?"

BUCK shook his head. "I make sure nobody knows where I'm going. That's the only way to protect a strike till it's yours on paper. Every miner knows that."

"Yes," Ames sighed. "The murderer knew it too. He knew you'd be left without an alibi if he timed things right... Tell me," he said, "exactly what did you do with Scotty that day you loaned him a boat?"

"Nothing much. He went with me to my blastport where I fueled the ship with my own fuel. I showed him what to watch out for, because the *Hellcat's* a tough boat to tow sometimes. Then we went back to the Standish port and Scotty fueled up, and we both went off together. We went out about fifty miles and stopped. Scotty took me aboard his ship and brought me back to my own port. Then he went back to where he'd space-anchored the *Hellcat* and took her in tow, I guess."

"Why such a complicated routine?"

"I don't know. I guess Scotty wanted to make sure I couldn't follow him. He was pretty careful, you know."

"Was anybody at the blastport when Scotty took you back?"

"Any witnesses, you mean? No. It was a Saturday night."

Ames sighed again. "When was the next time anyone saw you?"

"That night, about two hours later."

"Who?"

"Never mind who," said Buck. "Somebody saw me."

"All right," said Ames. "Can you count on that somebody to be a witness for you—to prove you returned?"

Buck nodded, and Ames noticed he avoided Sue's eyes.

"Not that this witness is too important," said Ames. "The prosecution could claim you'd followed Scotty before and knew where to find him. Then, when you were supposedly off on a prospecting trip, you went to his mine and killed him."

"Hell," said Buck, somberly, "you're my lawyer and you make out a case against me that's ten times as strong as the one that louse Whitley tried to cook up."

Ames stretched his long legs. He said, "It's the case I saw him getting ready to cook before your eyes...if you took the stand..."

Buck said, quietly, "How did you know all this?"

Ames replied, thoughtfully, "I knew you didn't have an alibi, or Whitley would never have tried to indict you. What's the sense of indicting a man who's going to bring an airtight alibi to his trial? So I knew you'd only hang yourself if you spoke...

"But I had another reason. I had to stop Whitley from trying the case then and there, which he would practically have done if he could have cornered you on the stand. Once your story was out—and spread through the town, as it would be—we'd have little chance to get an unprejudiced jury. Murchison's paper tried the indictment before it reached the Court; if you'd spoken, you'd have given *Twin-Sun* its chance to conduct the trial in its editorial columns." He looked at Sue as he added. "When I admitted the indictment, I stopped Whitley from turning it into a trial. You understand that now, I think?"

Presently, Buck said, "What about the trial? I still have no alibi. What am I going to say then?"

Ames seemed lost in thought. After awhile, he said, "I don't know. We're up against thorough opposition. You saw how the case began to unfold, with every detail in place, with every move of yours witnessed when it was necessary. I think we'll find witnesses at every point in this story. What I've got to do is follow the prosecution's trail and stop at each of these points, and analyze them carefully..."

"I've got to have some kind of action," Buck said.

Ames looked at Buck and saw the darkness in his face, and though he'd felt instinctively that Buck Wylie was a strong man, he understood how helpless he must feel. Ames looked at his watch and got up as the turnkey's footsteps echoed along the planking. "I'll be back tomorrow," he said. "Maybe something will break."

He thought of shaking hands with him, but Buck was staring out of the tiny window. When he and Sue left, Ames had the feeling that Buck had turned to look after them. Ames was surprised to find himself thinking what he felt was a curious thought, but he took his hand away from Sue's arm just the same.

THEY were almost at the outside door when Sue turned to Ames and said, "I'm sorry about the things I said. I'll never doubt you again." She took his hand and whispered, "I think you're a wonderful lawyer."

"Thanks," said Ames, feeling hot and cold.

It happened instantly. As Ames opened the door for Sue, the flexiglass shivered and fell out. It seemed to melt away from a spot, where, for an instant, a neat little hole had appeared. Ames would have stood there, fascinated by the thing, but Sue Wylie grabbed him and pushed him against a wall. The next moment the air danced in shimmering, conical form and a hole appeared in the wall where Ames had been standing a moment before. It was about a quarter inch in diameter, with edges that smoldered…about the size a Foster II heat pistol would make.

Later, when Ames had finished with the guards who had come running to the scene, and when he had a chance to draw his breath, he said to Sue, "I guess someone else decided I was a good lawyer."

They were very quiet as they walked along, going, as if by some silent agreement, toward where Ames lived, until Ames gathered courage and put it in words. "Will you have dinner with me tonight?"

She looked up at him as if she hadn't heard. "Tomorrow morning you'll take out a pistol permit," she said, her eyes clouded.

"We'll talk about it at dinner," Ames said.

"Dinner?" Sue repeated, musing.

"You're coming, aren't you?"

"Of course," she said. "Of course I am. I'm afraid to leave you alone now. You don't know this town. You don't know how capable of violence this sleepy little place can be." A little shiver ran through her. "You'll need someone to take care of you."

They were almost at Ames' house when the boy Willy came bounding down from the porch. "Mr. Ames!" he cried. "You just missed your friends. They left about five minutes ago."

"What friends?"

"You know—the men you sent to get your papers. They went in and took them. They said for me to tell you."

Ames didn't wait to hear the rest of it. He ran up the steps and into the house. When Sue followed a moment later, she found Ames in the midst of an office that looked like a hurricane had hit it. The bookshelves had been torn apart, a filing case had been opened and ransacked, the desk drawers lay on the floor. Papers and books lay everywhere.

Ames sat down on the floor and began going through a brown envelope. He searched through other papers before he got up. He didn't seem to be too worried about matters. He smiled wryly at Sue and said, "It wasn't much. It seems they found out that Judge Averill wanted me to present my credentials—"

"When was this?" Sue asked, puzzled. "Why did he ask for them?"

"This afternoon. I guess the judge didn't think I was much of a lawyer." Ames grinned as he surveyed the littered room, "Looks like there are two schools of thought on that, all right. Not only did they take a pot shot at me, but now they've stolen my credentials."

"But why?"

"Because if I don't have them over at the judge's tomorrow, I have a feeling Averill may bounce me off the case."

"But that's impossible. Buck needs a lawyer—he needs you!"

"Well," Ames said, "he could always order Lawyer Farley to take the case. Maybe your brother would like that."

"You mean you haven't a duplicate set of credentials?"

Sue said, slowly. "It'll be weeks before you can have another set shipped here!"

"I don't think so," Ames grinned.

"A thing like this might have been serious in other circumstances, but I'd say our friends missed the target again..." Even as he spoke he became thoughtful, and he had to remember to keep the grin alive because Sue was watching him. He thought to himself: *unless I've made the greatest mistake of all...*

CHAPTER FOUR

SHORTLY before noon the next day, Ames was seated in the living room of Judge Averill's home. He had begun by telling the judge that he could not present his credentials, and he had told him why. All the time he was speaking, the judge sat gravely, listening without once interrupting, until finally, when Ames had finished his short recital, his voice had dropped away until it was barely audible.

"Well, Mr. Ames," Averill said, after a moment or two, "I'd hardly know whether to believe you or not if I hadn't heard that you were shot at when you left the jail house yesterday. Why didn't you mention it?"

"I didn't think it mattered," Ames said. He opened the briefcase he had brought with him and took out a thick yellow scroll. "I didn't know what you'd think, sir," he said, "so I ethergraphed to New York to some friends of mine and asked them to vouch for me. I received this about an hour ago."

Averill sat up. "Ethergraphed to New York, did you?"

he said. He took the yellow scroll that was the graph and opened it. For several minutes thereafter he read in complete silence. Once or twice he paused to look at Ames. Finally, when he had finished, he let out a sigh and slowly lit a cigar. "I think, Mr. Ames," he said, "that I owe you an apology."

Ames felt his face growing red. He gulped and said nothing.

Averill blew smoke out. "Why didn't you tell me you were *that* Ames—the Terwilliger Ames of Consolidated?"

"Well, sir, I hardly thought…that is…"

"I see," said the judge. "You seem to be suffering from chronic modesty. Did you think your reputation hadn't reached Mirabello," and here Averill smiled, "or didn't you think an old country judge like me would bother to read the Law Review?"

He stood up and offered his hand to Ames. "Here," he said, leading Ames to one of the bookcases that lined the room, "every issue of the past eight years, and about thirty years more stored away in the attic." He pulled out several copies and thumbed through them, stopping at one. "*Corporate Liability and Recent Criminal Laws*," he read aloud, "*by Terwilliger Ames*," put the periodical down and snorted, "Why, I must have read a dozen of your articles. I never imagined that you—"

And here he looked at Ames curiously and asked, "But what *did* bring you out here, Ames? What makes a brilliant young lawyer with a system-wide reputation come to a place like Mirabello?"

"I don't know," Ames sighed. "I guess—" He smiled and threw up his hands. "One of these days I'll be glad to get together with you, sir, and discuss philosophies of living, but I confess right now I've so much on my mind I can't think straight." He added, "May I assume that I have your permission to continue with this case?"

Averill said, slowly, "I wish I knew whether you enjoy joking."

"Thank you, sir," Ames said, with evident relief, "but it was no joke for me a couple of hours ago, before I knew what you'd—" He stopped speaking, in sudden embarrassment.

"Before you knew I'd what?" asked the Judge.

"It doesn't matter, sir. I'm very tired; I'm talking too much."

"I see," said Judge Averill, reflectively. "You didn't know whether I'd accept this graph from your friends as evidence of competence? But why shouldn't I? Why not...unless you imagined I was persecuting you...or wanted you to give up this case?" Suddenly the judge looked directly at Ames and said, "You must have been wondering whether I was involved in what seems to be a plot to get you out of this case. All right, you needn't answer. You've every right to be careful after what's happened. But if you get into any trouble, and you decide you can trust me, come to me. Maybe I can help."

"Thank you, sir," Ames said, sincerely.

Later, when he had started the first leg of his long itinerary, Ames wondered whether he might not have to ask Judge Averill to postpone the trial. He had only ten days, hardly time enough to turn around in. He had a lot of things to do in that time.

HE returned home and changed into old clothes, and then he walked out to the edge of the town where the Standish blastport was.

The Standish port seemed out of place in Mirabello

City. It had something definitely—as Ames thought—big-time about it. It was a large, efficiently run port. Half the field was given over to the freighters that came to Mirabello for orium; the other half, or most of it, was used by the various miner craft. The miner craft were of all sizes and makes, from the ancient *Blakes* to fairly recent, slick beryllium jobs. They sat on the port aprons together, their holds open to the sun, their bows looking at the sky, as if impatient to be off again.

There were miners everywhere, talking, laughing, drinking. Their calling was a hard one, but it made men. The representatives of the orium companies knew that, and so did the crews from the freighters.

Ames walked around the port for awhile, taking in the hustle and hurry of the place, trying to feel its tempo before he undertook talking to any of the men who belonged there. He wound up, finally, at a bar, drinking Jovian rum. He spoke casually with the men on either side of him before he introduced Scotty's name.

Instantly the conversation ceased.

When Ames tried to open it again, the miner on his left said, "What are you after, Mr. Ames?"

Ames swallowed his drink. "How do you know my name?" he said.

The miner unfolded a copy of the *Twin-Sun*. The front page carried the story of Buck Wylie's indictment, but what got Ames' attention was a two-column picture of himself. It had evidently been taken on the street some time after the proceedings, for Sue Wylie's hand rested on his arm, where her picture had been cut away. The caption read: *T. Ames, The Man Who Defends Wylie.*

"Well," said Ames, "I'll tell you what I'm after. I wanted to talk to someone who knew Scotty Purdom. I wanted to find out what kind of a man he was."

One miner nodded to another, and the first one said, "Did I hear you say somethin' about buyin' the next round?"

It was seven or eight rounds later when Ames walked unsteadily back to his house. From the vast amount of anecdotage and lore he had listened to, he had come away with little. Scotty had been secretive to extremes; no one knew much about him. All kinds of rumors were rife—that Murchison had been only a quarter partner, or less, or more. That Buck had been on the verge of partnership with Scotty; that both had actually been partners in a new, secret venture; that Scotty had probably been killed accidentally but that Buck wouldn't talk until he had first protected the new claim legally. All agreed, however, in one particular—that John Murchison had loved Scotty and would do anything to get his revenge on the man who had murdered him.

Ames wrote it all down when he got home. He barely kept his eyes open until he finished, then he fell asleep on his desk.

When he woke, Sue Wylie was standing beside him, shaking him. He looked at the steaming pot of coffee she had prepared, and though he flushed, he drank it gratefully. "I'm immersing myself in the intimate details of the case," he explained, adding ruefully, "Maybe I got too immersed."

A little while later he went out again, heading for the editorial offices of the *Twin-Sun*. He had wanted to meet John Murchison, and now that he did, he spoke plainly. He found Murchison purposeful and straightforward. The big man offered him a chair as calmly as if he had been expecting Ames.

AMES said, "I see you've got my picture on the front page."

"You don't object to publicity, do you?" Murchison smiled. "A big New York lawyer like you should be used to it."

Ames couldn't help reacting. He flushed and said, "You might have mentioned the fact that I was shot at and had my office ransacked."

Murchison frowned, puzzled. He reached for a copy of the paper and opened it before Ames. "I see you didn't get past the front page, Mr. Ames," he said. "The *Twin-Sun* prints all the news—even when it's liable to be phony news."

Ames looked up from the paper. "You don't believe I was shot at?"

Murchison smiled. "I'm sure you were. I'm not sure who did the shooting."

"What do you mean?"

"I mean," said Murchison, calmly, "that your worthy client Buck Wylie could have had one of his men shoot at you."

"But why?"

"Need I explain?" Murchison smiled. "It isn't a bad idea to have a defense attorney shot at. It not only creates sympathy, but it seems to imply that there are—shall we say—extra-legal parties interested in the case? It's fine build-up to claim dark plots are afoot." He let his smile fade away. "On the other hand, Mr. Ames, there is always the possibility Wylie arranged the thing just to convince you. And there is still a third possibility. Care to hear it? It isn't pretty."

"By—all means."

"You'll know the answer to this one better than I."

Murchison leaned back in his swivel chair. "It may be that Buck Wylie doesn't like you, Mr. Ames. Maybe you've been asking him too many questions. Maybe you've made him feel uncomfortable enough for him to do something about it. Wylie's a man of action."

"I see," said Ames, rising to leave. "However, all these theories are based on the assumption that Wylie is guilty, aren't they?"

Murchison rose with him, leaning against the door. He nodded soberly. "He *is* guilty, Mr. Ames; make no mistake about that. You see, you don't know Wylie—but the more you investigate him, as I hope you will, the more you'll come to agree with me. But I'll tell you this: I am prepared to use every honest means at my disposal to see that Wylie pays the penalty for what he did to Scotty." He had pounded his fist on the desk as he spoke. Now, grimly, he added, "And I may even allow myself a little leeway in deciding which means are honest. Do we understand each other, Mr. Ames?"

"Somewhat, Mr. Murchison," Ames said. "Good afternoon, sir."

It was now close to five o'clock, and Ames went to the local ethergraph office. The dozens of minute details and impressions he had already gathered were buzzing around in his mind, and he couldn't make head nor tail of any of them. He needed someone to talk to, someone like Judge Averill. Sue Wylie would have been fine, but he preferred neutrals in cases like this. The only question now was whether Judge Averill was really a neutral. Ames muttered to himself, realizing that he was going in circles. He hadn't been able to make a single one of his decisions stick for any length of time.

He walked into the office of System Ethergraph, Ltd.

and asked for the manager. A small, dapper man came out to see Ames.

Ames said, "I think you remember me. I was here for several hours early this morning." The manager nodded, and Ames said, "I have another message I want you to transmit to New York and—"

"Won't one of our clerks do, Mr. Ames?"

"I thought you'd be interested in this message," said Ames.

The manager raised his eyebrows. "Certainly, Mr. Ames."

Ames waited until the manager poised his stylus. "To the System Ethergraph, Ltd.; Central Office, New York," Ames dictated. "Attention Legal Dept. Notice is hereby served that the undersigned is filing criminal and civil actions against your company, as per Communications Statutory Laws, Section 885. Will charge that the manager of the Mirabello branch office did willfully reveal the contents of an ethergraph addressed—Terwilliger Ames."

"Is that all, Mr. Ames?"

"I think so."

"The charges will be twenty-four dollars. May I thank you for your patronage?"

AMES paid and left, feeling tremendously relieved. He had satisfied himself that it had been the manager and not Judge Averill, who had told Murchison of Ames' standing in New York. The graph itself was worthless; he had no proof and no case, but the manager's calm demeanor in the face of a serious charge had told Ames what he wanted to know.

A moment later Ames laughed savagely at himself. It was still possible that *both* the manager and Averill had told

Murchison! He was letting the details entangle him. He consulted his memorandum and headed for the Bureau of Meteorology. He would stay with the details. It was the only way he knew how to work.

At the Bureau he asked for the chief clerk and explained what he wanted. Were the files of the Bureau open for public inspection?

"I'll be glad to be of service, Mr. Ames," said the clerk. "Can you be more specific about which files you want?"

"How do you know my name?" said Ames.

"Why, your picture was in the paper today, Mr. Ames."

Ames nodded. "I want to consult the files on weather conditions for the past two months," he said.

"Can you tell me which areas you are interested in?"

"I don't know," said Ames. "Suppose I were a miner. What areas would I have to watch out for, say, the tenth and eleventh of this month?"

"I can't say anything offhand, Mr. Ames. The miners here are scattered around for hundreds of thousands of miles, at the very least. The main asteroid belt is over six million miles long, and there are miners all through it. I'd say, roughly, that there were at least two or three areas that had storms during the days you mention."

"All right," said Ames, wearily.

"Let's get the files and see exactly how many areas there were and what they were."

An hour later Ames left. There had turned out to be four storm areas, all widely scattered, and none of them violent, though the one at the so-called Double Horn had lasted several weeks. Ames had carefully written down every bit of information.

On his way home he stopped at the library and spent some time with *Ghort's Atlas of the Forty-first System Group*, of which Mirabello was a member. He checked the distances of each storm area from Mirabello and added them to his notes.

When he got home, Sue Wylie was there. She was wearing an apron and she had prepared dinner. "Tonight you'll be my guest," she smiled. Ames could see that she was waiting for him to tell her what he had done that day, but he waited until he had finished eating. He was too tired to eat much.

He sat down on the couch in his little living room when he was done. There was a package lying on a table, and atop it lay an envelope. Curious, Ames looked at Sue and opened the envelope. Inside was a folded certificate for a pistol permit. It had been signed by Judge Averill.

"When did you see Averill?" he asked.

"This afternoon."

"Did you have any trouble getting this?"

"No. He said it was a little irregular for someone to apply for another's pistol permit, but he said he'd make an exception for you." She said, taking a cigarette, "He seems to have changed in the way he feels about you. You haven't told me a thing."

Ames said nothing. He opened the package and his eyes popped. "What do you think I'm going to do with this?" he exclaimed. He gingerly removed the heat pistol and holstered belt that were in the package. He examined it, looked at the permit, then said, "This is a Foster IV! It's practically a portable cannon!"

"They're the only kind my brother owns. I told him what happened yesterday and he had one of his men bring it in." She hesitated before she added, "Buck expected you today, you know."

"I had a lot to do today," said Ames.

"Aren't you going to tell me about it?"

Ames said, "I don't know." He put the gun away and said, with his back to the girl, "Tell me, Miss Wylie, what would you say…" But he broke off, sat down again, and took out his notebook. "I'll give you what I've got," he said. He read his notes, summarizing his activities. When he finished, he said, "What do you think?"

"May I ask some questions?"

"I wish you would. It may help me."

"Why did you write down all those absurd things you heard at the Standish port? Why should you be interested in rumors?"

AMES said, slowly, "Because I'm not sure yet what is rumor and what is fact. I've got to see everything for myself. I've got to wade through an enormous mass of facts in the hope that one will mean something. I don't know how to judge the things I know now."

"Why did you hunt up the weather and those distances?"

"Well," said Ames, "there's one remarkable thing about what I do know—Scotty's asking your brother for his boat. Scotty mined the same place for ten years. Weren't there storms there before? What did he do those times? Is it possible that he was engaged in mining a new place—a place where he really needed an extra boat—as he hadn't needed any with his old mine?

"You see," Ames continued, looking at the girl, "suppose we assume that there is some truth to the rumor that Buck and Scotty recently entered into a partnership to work a new mine together. I don't know why they would—but if they did, it explains a lot. For instance, that might be the reason Scotty needed another boat—the new mine being in a dangerous area, while the Silver Spoon obviously wasn't. That would explain why he asked Buck for a boat, of all people. Third, it might tell us where Buck was those six days he says he went prospecting.

"But best of all," Ames said, slowly, "it would provide a better motive for Murchison's determination to be revenged on your brother. I somehow can't swallow that business of his being so devoted to Scotty—or of anyone being very devoted to him. He wasn't the kind of man that other men felt strongly about, one way or another. It may very well be that Murchison hates Buck more than he loved Scotty—because he knew, maybe from Scotty, that he was being supplanted…"

"Then you don't believe Buck told you the truth?"

"I didn't say that," Ames began. "He may—"

"You think Buck killed Scotty, don't you?"

"Not necessarily," Ames said. "I'm just theorizing, but even if the suppositions are true, Scotty might have been killed accidentally; If such a thing had happened, Buck might be afraid to tell the truth because of his record. He might have tried to protect himself by bringing back Scotty's boat and attempting to destroy it, which again points to the theory of the new mine.

"You see, Scotty's Silver Spoon was a secret for ten years—so obviously a boat could be left there without fear of its being spotted from space. But if the new mine didn't afford such protection, it would have to be brought back and destroyed…"

He stopped speaking, regarding Sue carefully. He sat down closer to her and said, quietly, "Shall I continue?"

She was smoking very nervously as he spoke. She nodded.

"That's why I'm checking the weather and the

distances," Ames resumed. "Scotty left on the tenth. If I could find an area for which the Meteorological Bureau had issued warnings somewhere around that time, I might be able to get an idea of where Scotty had gone. It couldn't have been far if he was due back in eight days, fully loaded. Furthermore, if Buck was gone six days, he would have had plenty of time to make the round trip there and back."

"You've listed four areas," Sue said. "Do any of them fit?"

"Possibly. I can't be sure until I can compare the speeds of both the boats that figure in it... I wonder if you'd do me a favor?"

"If I can."

"Will you take me to Buck's blastport tomorrow? I want to go over the ground, maybe talk to some of his men."

"All right, I will."

Ames sat there, undecided. Presently he asked, "What are you thinking about?"

She was looking at a picture across the room. "I'm thinking I'm glad you're being so methodical about this, because I know you'll get to the bottom of it."

Ames took a deep breath. He went back to the couch, saying, "And you're not afraid of what I'll find when I hit bottom?"

She didn't answer. She continued sitting there, bemused, and Ames made no effort to continue the conversation. He took the volume he had been reading and stretched out. Once she said to him, "You're very tired. Why don't you go to sleep?" Ames said something about having to continue his studies and kept reading...

When he woke up, several hours later, the room was in

semi-darkness. The wall clock told him he had been asleep for three hours. Only a table lamp was lit, and across the room, curled up in the large chair, Sue Wylie lay asleep. The Foster gun lay on a chair that she had pulled up near her.

Ames sat up, and his coat fell off him. She had covered him with it and undertaken to keep guard over him. He didn't know what to do. He didn't want to wake her at that hour, and he was too embarrassed to think of asking her to use his bedroom. In the end he covered her up with his coat and laid the gun down beside him on the couch. If there was any protecting to be done, he thought, he would do it...

CHAPTER FIVE

OVER breakfast the next morning, Ames said, "You shouldn't have stayed here last night."

"My reputation, you mean?" Sue smiled. "It'll stand it."

"I mean there was no necessity for it, not only because I'm perfectly capable of taking care of myself, but because there was no danger of anything happening."

She swallowed, then said, "You seem very sure of that."

"It stands to reason. Whoever shot at me two days ago has had innumerable opportunities to do so again. It hasn't been tried, and I don't think it will be."

"Why?" she said, sharing the bacon with him. "Change of plan?"

"I think so. Whoever took that shot at me was a pretty reckless sort. He did it in broad daylight, in the heart of the town. Well, that kind of direct action doesn't jibe too well with the indirect action of stealing my credentials, does it? The man who shot at me would have tried again, being the sort he is—but whoever it was that thought of stopping me by stealing my credentials must have ordered him to layoff." He added, his mouth full, "I think they're laying off because they're curious. They want to know what I'll do. Or maybe they think they can outwit me. Flatters them more."

Sue observed, "That doesn't sound like Buck, then if he were behind it, he'd have you shot. He likes action."

Ames dropped his fork. "How—how did you know?" he stammered. "You—"

"I looked through your notes after you fell asleep," said Sue, pouring the coffee. She pushed a cup towards Ames and looked into his eyes. "I thought maybe you were sparing me something, and I wanted to know. I read the account of your conversation with Murchison, where he said he thought Buck might have had you shot at."

Ames stirred his coffee. "You don't think so?"

"Not at all. Not a chance of it being true."

Ames said, "You remember the hole that shot left? About a quarter of an inch—from a Foster II." Sue nodded, and Ames said, "Yesterday Buck gave you a Foster IV to give me. I noticed he told you he didn't have any other kind of gun. It might have been an indirect way of letting me know that none of his men had shot at me, because they would have used Foster's IV's. What about it?"

She put her coffee down and shook her head. "I don't know where you keep it all. Your head is like some huge storeroom, with room for all kinds of odds and ends…and a little worthless junk too, I'm afraid…just a little."

"You know," said Ames curiously, "that's almost exactly

what a professor of mine told me once, except that he said my head was like a library with a terribly disordered filing system…" He smiled at the reminiscence. "Comes to the same thing;" he mused, "but I'll be damned if I can think of any other way to think a thing out."

"Were you a good lawyer in New York?"

"How do you know I'm from New York?"

"Silly. It's in the *ex libris* of all your books."

"Oh," said Ames. "I was pretty good, I guess…"

They left shortly afterward, though not without an argument about the necessity of taking along the gun. Ames didn't take it, standing by his analysis. "Here lies Terwilliger Ames," Sue said. "Still standing by his analysis." But Ames noticed she didn't press matters too much; she was learning to trust his judgment.

Sue had called Buck's *arrando*—it was a Martian word that meant, roughly, a ranch—early that morning, and a gyro was waiting for them when they reached Standish port.

"This is Sour Tom," said Sue, introducing Ames to a lanky, burnt man whose face looked as if a smile would disfigure it. "Tom's going to take us out to the place."

"Don't know if I can get clearance off this danged port," Tom scowled. "Holdin' everything up waitin' for the danged mail freight to blow in. I hope you won't mind waitin' a bit, Miss Sue?"

Sue smiled. "Not at all, Tom. I guess you must be expecting your monthly batch of magazines on that danged mail freighter."

The least bit of a grin crept into the corners of Tom's mouth. "Yep," he said, sheepishly. "Never could fool you, Miss Sue."

A FEW minutes later the Standish port sirens went off with fantastic vigor—a signal used only for crashes and the arrival of mail. When the individual vessels that dotted the apron and the field joined in it meant mail, and a few minutes of utter chaos. People ran about excitedly, shouting to each other in vain efforts to pierce the din, and the control tower broke out a halyard of signal flags. And then the mail freighter flashed in the sky overhead, her silver hull gleaming in the sunlight, her fore rockets easing her off, spluttering with self-importance. Down she came in a graceful arc, landing as softly as a bird...

Fifteen minutes later, Sour Tom came hurrying towards them, a bulky package under his arm. There was a happy light in his eyes, but his face had no share in it. "This way, folks," he sang out, leading them to the south apron. They were off in a few minutes.

The gyro was a fairly large plane, evidently used a great deal to carry supplies from the town to the *arrando*.

Tom got it up to three thousand feet, set the controls and opened the package. "Ahhh," he breathed, contentedly, riffling the pages of one of the magazines. "I'm halfway into the dangest serial I ever laid my eyes on." Ames glanced at the cover of the magazine. It was *Rip-Snorting Wild West Stories*.

The flight lasted almost an hour-and-a-half, taking them deep into country Ames had never seen before. The earth that lay under their wings was green and lovely, and everything flourished in its soil with unbelievable disregard for horticultural laws. Its streams were like bits of gold ribbon, its fields like gardens. Deeper in were jungles, warmed by hot springs that coursed a few feet under the soil, and then, off to the west, the Grey Mountains rose, the peaks like burnished copper above the shadowed slate of the range.

Ames drank it all in, his eyes fastened on the scenes that unfolded before him, but his mind was occupied with other thoughts. Once Sue said to him, "I haven't been out this way in a long time," and he nodded, wondering what lay behind her words.

The Wylie *arrando* stood atop a plateau that climbed out of wild, desolate country. It was a large place, comprising more than a dozen buildings. Farther along the plateau was another group of structures, but these were open-topped sheds that stored orium. Sour Tom brought the gyro down in a small, fenced-off field near the main house, where we led them.

The main house was a two-storied affair with wide piazzas and long expanses of glassine walls. Oaks and aspens surrounded it, and a carefully attended garden ran all around the place. There were paths that led to the other houses, some of which Ames guessed were for the men Buck Wylie employed. And there were barns and stables, for the fields on the far edge of the plateau were cultivated, and the luxuriant range was grazing land for horses and cattle.

Ames hadn't expected anything like it. It wasn't so much the evidence of great wealth and luxury—and of good taste—that surprised him, but the definite effort that had been made to combine the best features that Mirabello offered with nostalgic contributions from home. He breathed the air in deeply and looked about the place with shining eyes. This was no *arrando*; it was a magnificent estate. Ames doubted whether its equal existed on Mirabello.

Some of the men, who were busy around the barns and shed, waved to Sue from their tasks. When they reached the flagstone path, Tom said, "See you later, I hope, Miss Sue. Pleasure, Mr. Ames." He motioned toward the house and his face darkened. "Waitin' for you," he said.

As they went through the gardens and approached the house, Ames saw whom Tom had meant. There was a woman standing on the piazza near the front door. Two Irish setters lay quietly at her feet, and then, seeing Sue, they rose and started running toward her when a sharp word from the woman halted them and brought them back.

SHE was quite a beautiful woman, Ames thought, when he was introduced to her. "Miss Morales, Mr. Ames," she said, quietly. "Mr. Ames is Buck's attorney, Lola." She was in her early thirties, Ames judged, but age meant nothing in a woman like her. She was exotic, with dark, burning, hard eyes, and jet-black hair that lay in braids over her bare shoulders. She wore a simple peasant dress that must have cost a great deal, Ames imagined, because it was made entirely of fiberglass, and the brilliant colors suited her olive skin.

"How is Buck?" Lola Morales asked.

"He's fine," said Sue. "He asked for you yesterday."

"I'm going to see him this afternoon," said Lola. "I tried to get away yesterday, but I had to supervise the paymaster." She issued a call to the dogs. "I must talk to the foreman now," she said before she left. "If you want anything, call Pedro." Then, just before she went down the stairs, she asked, casually, "Does Buck know you're here?"

Sue hesitated briefly, then said, "No; we came out quite suddenly."

A few minutes later, sitting under a huge umbrella and

sipping tall glasses of iced *juno*, Ames said, quietly, "Is Lola the witness your brother meant? I mean the time I asked him who had seen him that Saturday night and he wouldn't answer." Sue nodded. Ames said, "I guess she's also the reason you don't live here anymore."

Sue said, "Let's walk around a bit, shall we?"

"Sure," Ames agreed. "And you can tell me about Lola. I'd like to know more about her." He flushed horribly as Sue darted a glance at him. "I mean," he mumbled, "we may need her as a witness and...and..." Suddenly he blurted, "Excuse me, Miss Wylie, but you're a fool if you think any man would look twice at another woman with you around!" And having said it, he stood stock-still, seemingly paralyzed on the stairs, shocked by what he had uttered.

"Why, Mr. Ames!" said Sue. "What a gallant thing to say!" She looked up at his lean, embarrassed face and smiled. "But don't you think it would have sounded better if you had called me Sue—with such a speech?"

"All right," Ames gulped, "but that goes both ways."

"You mean you want me to call you Terwilliger?" she laughed.

The color in his face deepened. "Call me Ames," he said.

She took his hand and led him. They walked then, going through the stocked sheds and well-equipped barns, talking to the men. Once they saw Lola. She was returning to the house. As if by common agreement they dropped their handclasp. A little while later, a large, stylish gyro rose from the field and Sue said, "That's Lola going now."

It was almost noon when Ames looked at his watch. The time had sped by quickly. "We've spent too long a time here already," Ames said. "I've got most of what I came here for. Now I'll see if I can get the rest of it." He thought a moment, then asked, "This Sour Tom likes you a lot, I know. Does he trust you? I mean, I thought from the way he looked at Lola that he sort of was on your side. Am I right?"

"I think so," Sue said, searchingly. "Ames, you're not thinking of doing anything against Buck, are you?"

"No," said Ames. He let a little sigh escape him. "I told you I've got most of what I came for. Do you know what that was? I wanted to see the kind of place Buck Wylie lived in, to see if I could perhaps understand the kind of life he leads. Well, I've seen it. Buck told me had made enough money for one lifetime and I believe him. He has everything a man could want here. He lives like a prince, but he hasn't flaunted his wealth here. A man like that wouldn't kill for money..." He met Sue's eyes and said, "So you see, I've decided that he didn't kill Scotty. I've quite decided..."

"But what about your theory that it might have been an accident?"

"I don't know," Ames said, thoughtfully. "That's a bridge I'll come to yet, but it'll be a lot easier to cross than this might have been. Right now I want to see Tom and have a talk with him. Do you know where he is?"

"I think so," Sue smiled. "Follow me."

She led Ames to the farthermost barn and went in. She called out once, "Tom!" A minute later, Tom came sliding down from a hayloft, his magazine carefully folded to keep his place.

"TOM," said Sue, looking at him, "Mr. Ames here is Buck's lawyer. You know that. Mr. Ames is trying to save

Buck's life. He's got some things he wants to ask about—maybe some personal things about Buck. Whatever they are, I want you to tell him the truth. Don't keep anything back. Do you understand me, Tom?"

"Dang it all," said Tom, disgusted. "You don't have to go makin' a danged speech like that at me. I'd cut my left arm off for you, Miss Sue, you know that." He added, to Ames, "I'm left-handed, you notice."

Ames said, "Do you know anything about Mr. Wylie's boats—the ones he carries orium in?"

"Guess I do, if anybody does. Any one in particular?"

"The *Hellcat*, I think it's called. Do you know anything about the speed she can make?"

"Guess I do. Guess that danged boat could do plenty."

"Can you make that a little more specific? For instance, do you think she could do half a million miles in three days?"

Sour Tom scratched his head. "Guess she could. You see, Mr. Ames, the *Hellcat's* a funny boat. She acts up every now an' then, and we have her over at Hank Miller's more than she's here. Spends more time in his repair sheds—"

"Who is Hank Miller?"

"Why, Hank's the feller that runs the big Miller Rocket Sheds just outside Riverdale. He's got a way with the *Hellcat*, as Buck says. She spends more time in his sheds gettin' her machinery straightened out than she does pullin' orium. Mighty funny boat, she is."

"Do you think you could let me have a look at her?"

"Don't see how I could," said Tom, "seein' as how she's been seized by the law and put in the pound. She and Scotty's boat, both."

"You mean the *Hellcat's* been impounded?" said Ames, puzzled. "It doesn't make sense. Why should they impound her?"

"Guess maybe they figured they'd have a try at her Berry gauge."

"Why? What is a Berry gauge?"

Tom shifted his weight from one foot to the other. "That's the thingamabob that keeps track of the fuel and multiplies that by the time and I don't know what else and adds up the mileage the ship makes. It's a mighty handy gadget."

"You mean," said Ames, eagerly, "that by going through that gauge one can tell how far a ship's been?"

"That's right."

"How far back does it go? I mean, suppose one day I did a hundred miles, and the next day another hundred, and the third day I did fifty miles—how many of those trips would it keep a record of?"

"All of 'em, unless you bust open her seal and started her over again. That danged Berry can go into billions, I guess, with each separate start and finish marked plain from the next. Course, only a licensed mechanic like Hank's allowed to bust the seal—that's in case of an accident, so the seal will be intact if they need to investigate."

"Let me see if I understand you, Tom," said Ames. There was an odd look in his eyes. "The seal can only be opened by licensed people because in case of accident it might be necessary to find out where the ship had been? In fewer words, if the seal were intact, one could practically reconstruct a ship's voyage?"

"That's right."

"But suppose I were a criminal and I wanted to hide where I'd been? What would prevent me from breaking the seal myself?"

"You can't break it," said Tom, shaking his head. "The Berry gauge's made of alumalloy all the way through, includin' the seal. We've had wrecks that left nothin' but dust of the ship, but the Berry gauge was there, tickin' away, alive and cheerful. You can't touch 'em without a special nitro key, and you can't git a key without bein' licensed."

"Did Buck have such a license?"

Tom snorted. "Must be less than a dozen men in Mirabello got one of them licenses. Hank's got one, but where would Buck get one?"

"Do you know if Buck had such a key, perhaps?"

"Hell, no—they're harder to git than the license!"

"All right," said Ames. "Why couldn't a criminal burn out the entire gauge—just tear it out of the ship altogether?"

TOM shook his head again and regarded Sue judiciously. "Guess you ain't never been in a minin' craft, Mr. Ames," he said, "That Berry gauge is fixed right smack in the center of the control board. If you tried to take it out, you'd wreck the ship. Ain't nobody can git one of them gadgets out and still have a ship—not even Hank Miller. No, sir…"

Ames leaned against a fence and remained silent, his face screwed up. Sue said, quietly, "What's the matter, Ames?"

Ames let his breath out with a sigh. "I'm not sure," he said. "You remember the testimony established that Scotty's boat was seized while it was circling near Grey Mountain—and it had supposedly just returned from a voyage. From what Tom says, the Berry gauge in that boat and in Buck's boat too, for that matter, must be intact. If that's so, the authorities should be able to reconstruct the last voyage of both the boats and—"

"Excuse me, Mr. Ames," Tom interrupted. "That don't necessarily follow. You could outfox that danged gadget easy enough. Say you aimed to go someplace a hundred thousand miles out, and you didn't want it to show up on the gauge. Well, all you got to do is go out there roundabout-like, addin', say, fifty thousand, and come back the same way—and that's what the gauge would show."

"I see," said Ames, lapsing into silence again.

"Course, that's only if you was up to somethin'," Tom explained. "That's why the authorities havin' Buck's and Scotty's gauges don't mean nothin' to 'em. Scotty was so sly he'd be sure to go roundabout no matter where he was goin'—and I guess Buck'd come back nice and roundabout himself, so the danged gauges ain't worth a—"

"What do you mean by that?"

"By what?"

"By saying Buck would come back roundabout," said Ames, his eyes fixed on Tom. "You sound as if you thought he'd done it."

Tom hitched his trousers up leisurely, eyeing Sue. "I ain't sayin' what I think, Mr. Ames. I ain't thought about it. All I got to say is, if Buck done it, he must've had a danged good reason…"

Ames took careful note of the way Tom had kept glancing at Sue as he spoke, but he said nothing about it, biding his time. "Tom," he said, "There's just one more thing I want to ask you about. Were you here during the twenty-fourth—the day Buck got back from his prospecting trip?" He added, "That was the same day they found Scotty's boat circling around Grey Mountain, remember?"

"Yes, sir, I was here. I remember Buck come in just before noon that day."

"Did he go out again during the rest of the day?"

"Can't say," said Tom, laconically.

"Why not? You were here all day."

"Can't say," Tom repeated.

Sue said, quietly, "I want you to say, Tom. For my sake."

TOM looked at her as if he hoped she might change her mind. Then he shifted his weight again and said, slowly, "I don't know, and that's the truth. Buck was dead tired when he come in, and he just plumped down into bed and went to sleep—so offhand, I'd figure he couldn't have gone out again that day. On the other hand," he said, hesitantly, "along about evenin', just before I went into town, I decided I'd have a quick look around the place. The other hands had all gone into town, and with Buck asleep, I figured it might be a good idea.

"Well, I went over to the orium sheds, and I was danged amazed to see the *Hellcat* sittin' there in the port. I hadn't seen her come in, and I didn't know how she'd gotten there. The other rocketeers around the place had gone into town the night before, and there wasn't anybody here but Buck who could've brought her in, and he was asleep. I figured Scotty must've brought her back and gone away without me seein' him.

"Well, I went over to the main house and told Lola about it and she said she'd tell Buck. The next mornin' Buck woke me up and asked *me* about the *Hellcat*. I told him what I knew, and he said he'd been asleep all that time. He seemed about as surprised as I was. Well, about an hour later, who comes flyin' in here but the Colonial

Attorney. That was the first we knew about Scotty's boat havin' been found the night before.

"Seems the C.A. had found out Buck'd lent Scotty the *Hellcat* and all the rest of it and he asked a lot of questions. Buck told him he didn't know nothin' about it. When the C.A. asked him who'd brought the *Hellcat* back, with Scotty missin', Buck just looked blank. The next mornin' they come here and arrested Buck."

"Thanks, Tom," said Ames, somberly. He took out his little book and added some notes to the ones he had already written. His face was dark as he said to Sue, "I think that's about all we can do here. It's still pretty much of a dead end."

Sue shook hands with Tom, and Tom said, "You wanted me to tell, didn't you, Miss Sue?"

"Yes, Tom. No matter how it looks, we know Buck didn't do it. The only way we can help him is by uncovering the whole truth."

"Well, then, Miss Sue, there's one thing more."

"You mean there's something you haven't told us?"

Tom nodded briefly. "Guess so. You see, Buck lent Scotty the *Hellcat* once before, about five, six weeks ago."

"What?" cried Ames.

"It's the truth. Nobody seems to know about it. I guess Buck don't even know that I knew. The other hands thought the *Hellcat* was over at Hank Miller's, but I knew Scotty had it."

"Good Lord!" Ames exclaimed softly. "Then the *Hellcat* had made that trip before! If there was some way of checking..." He broke off. "Tom, how far are we from Hank Miller's?"

"About an hour up yonder."

"I want you to take me there," said Ames, tensely.

"Sue, you'd better go back to Mirabello. I don't know how long I'll be."

"I'll wait here for you…at least until Lola gets back…"

He looked down at her sad, frightened face and he wanted to kiss her, but being the kind of man he was, he flushed and said, "See you…"

CHAPTER SIX

TOM flew Ames in the gyro. In something less than an hour they passed over Riverdale, a small, sprawling town that reminded Ames of an ancient French hamlet in Brittany. He was greatly surprised, therefore, to see the huge repair sheds that flanked Riverdale from the east, for they looked as if they belonged to a great industrial center. Four fat stacks belched green smoke into the warm noon air, and the ground for miles around was torn and blackened with rocket blasts. The repair sheds, of transparent, corrugated *bytly-metal*, distorted the forms of the several ships that lay in them, and the place hummed with activity.

Tom landed the gyro right in the middle of the plant. Without going into the office he led Ames down the length of a shed, past helmeted men who were repairing a set of rocket tubes on a mining craft. At the far end of the shed, in a sort of fenced-off area, sat a middle-aged man in overall trousers and shirtsleeves. He seemed oblivious to the noise around him as he adjusted the tail fins on a model of an I. P. destroyer.

"Howdy, Tom," he smiled, shaking hands. He adjusted his glasses with an inquiring look at Ames, meanwhile talking to Tom. "Anything new over at the place? That Lola high-handin' it over everyone with Buck out of the way? You hear any thing about—"

"Dang it all," Tom said, sourly, "you'v always got time for gossip, Hank. This here's Mr. Ames, Buck's lawyer."

"Thought I recognized the face," said Miller. He wiped his hands on his trousers and offered one to Ames. "Pleased to meet up with you, Mr. Ames. Sure got a lot of trouble on your hands, don't you?"

"That's what I came to see you about, Mr. Miller. I thought perhaps you could help me." He looked around and held his hands out. "Is there someplace here where we can talk without this noise?"

"Sure," said Miller, smiling. He threw a canvas cover over the model and grabbed Tom's hand, leading them out through a side door.

"Talk, talk!" Tom growled. "All you ever do 'round here."

"Got to keep up with the news, Tom," Miller said, merrily. He led them through the yards and across a road, where, atop a slight hill, a small, neatly painted bungalow stood. He motioned both men to lounge chairs under a gaily-colored umbrella and said, "What can I do for you, Mr. Ames? Glad to be of service, if I can."

Ames said, slowly, "Tom here says you and Buck have always been good friends."

"Sure," said Miller. "Fine fellow, that Buck. Wasn't what you might call the friendly type, but a fine, hard workin' lad. Hated to see him get mixed up in something as dirty as that. Trouble with him was he didn't pay enough attention to the things right—"

"Mr. Ames," Tom scowled, "If you let him, Hank'll keep talkin' on any subject till he falls asleep in that chair.

Now look here, Hank, Mr. Ames ain't got the rest of the day, I don't think."

Ames said, "Mr. Miller, you were saying that you thought Buck was all right in your opinion. He was also a good customer of yours?"

"My best, maybe. Had four boats, and liked to keep 'em in good workin' order. Why, I remember the time…" He caught Tom's disgusted glance and stopped. "Sure," he said. "Fine customer."

"Did you ever do any work on the Berry gauges in his boats?"

"Berry gauges? Now, let me see. I do remember his bringing in the little one, the one with the Spanish name— *Gaucho*, that's it. Had some trouble with it not registering, 'bout seven months ago."

"Is that all?"

"Uh-huh. Of course, I'd know, because Buck always liked me to have a hand 'a tinkerin' with his boats. Said I had a way with them, and he wouldn't let my boys near them. Scotty—that's funny, my bringing up Scotty and Buck being accused of killing him—now, Scotty was the same way, always wantin' me to work on his boat. Now, there's a man who was always foolin' around with his Berry gauge—"

"You also took care of Scotty's boat? Regularly?"

"Sure. I take care of about ninety per cent of the mining boats in Mirabello. Course I don't give 'em all my personal attention."

"You were saying," Ames said, "Scotty was always—"

"Excuse me," Miller interrupted. "Just remembered something about that other question you asked me. Funny, my forgetting something like that, with me thinking about it only the other day, when I read in the paper they'd arrested Buck. He had the *Hellcat* in here about five weeks ago—asked me to set the Berry gauge on her back to zero."

"He brought the Hellcat here himself?"

"Sure. Who else—oh, I guess you mean did maybe one of his rocketeers bring her in? No, it was Buck all right. Funny, you askin'—"

"And all he did was ask you to set the gauge back to zero? He didn't ask you to give him a reading on it? He didn't want to know what the last figures on the gauge were?"

MILLER laughed. "You're way ahead of me, Mr. Ames. I'm tryin' to tell you. The day he came down here, Scotty was here, too. Scotty'd just come back from a trip and he wanted me to fix his Berry gauge, same as always. Well, Scotty seemed a heap more interested in Buck's gauge than Buck himself was. I guess even if Buck had wanted to find out what was on the gauge, he wouldn't have had a chance. Scotty kept him tied up in conversation all the time I was workin' on that gauge of Buck's."

"And Buck never asked you what was on it?"

"I'm comin' to it, Mr. Ames. No, Buck never asked me. Now, the way I work on a Berry gauge—keeping it ethical—I just open it up and spin the hell out of the dials, mixing 'em up. It's none of my business what's on 'em. And that's what I would have done that time, too, if Bax Murchison hadn't asked me to take special note of the reading."

Ames sucked his breath in audibly. "Murchison asked you that?"

"Yep. Asked me once and I said I wouldn't. Then he pulled out a batch of papers showing me Buck's criminal record, and he said he was checkin' up on Buck because the paper was doin' a big story on him. He wanted to know what Buck was up to."

"So you gave him the reading?" Ames asked, softly.

"Well, I don't do things that way. Course, I didn't know Buck had a record, but it still made no difference to me and I said no. The next day Murchison came back. He had a legal paper from Whitley, the Colonial Attorney, givin' me full authority to do what Murchison asked.

"Well, I didn't have the *Hellcat* in my sheds and I wasn't expecting her, so there wasn't anything I could do, paper or no. Then, about three days later—I'll be danged if Buck didn't bring that boat in! I wanted to tell him what I had to do, but Murchison had said if I breathed a word of it, he'd have the law on me…"

Hank Miller gestured with his hands. "What could I do? I had that danged paper, so I gave Murchison the readings. I thought it was a dirty trick at the time, but three days ago, when I picked up the paper and I saw what Buck'd done—why, I understood that Murchison had only been trying to do a public service. Understand me, I'm not sayin' a personal word against Buck; I liked him and I still do. At the same time, I've got to admit that Murchison knew what he was doin'. He must have known about that secret partnership Buck and Scotty were goin' into, and he was afraid, knowing Buck's record—"

Ames broke in. "What do you know about that secret partnership?"

"Well," Miller hemmed, "I guess I don't know much more than I've heard around. I get to see a lot of people even out here—"

"Gossip," said Tom, scowling. "Pack of old women. Craziest thing I ever heard of, Buck bein' partners with that cooty old Scotty."

"Nothin' wrong with gossip," said Miller, stoutly. "What are we doing right now but gossiping? Course, I wouldn't say anything about that whole business—haven't up to now—except that now that you bring it up, why, it's all coming out soon enough anyway, so I guess it's no secret anymore. You're a lawyer, Mr. Ames. Do you think I still need to keep quiet about the reading I gave Murchison?"

"I'LL tell you about that in a minute," said Ames, quietly. "Do you remember what that legal paper said? Did it say specifically that you were to give Murchison Buck's Berry gauge readings?"

"No, it just said I was to do what Murchison asked."

"Tell me, Mr. Miller, do you have any idea where the *Hellcat* had been just before Buck brought her in?" He added, "Or who had used her?"

"No, I don't recall. I guess Buck had her out on a trip. The last big figures on the gauge were around two hundred thousand, but I might be off a good bit, just tryin' to guess at it."

"Has Whitley been here to see you since that time?"

"Not since nor ever before. Never spoke to the man."

"One last question, please," Ames said. "A few minutes ago you said something about Scotty always having you work on his Berry gauge. Exactly what did you do to his gauge?"

"Shift her back to zero," Miller smiled, shaking his head. "I've never known a man like him. Everybody figured his gauge didn't show a thing anyway, with him probably goin' to his mine every which way. But just the same, at the end of every trip, he'd bring his boat in here and have me shift the Berry back to zero."

He shook his head again. "You want to know something, Mr. Ames? I'm not sayin' anything against him, him bein' dead somewhere and gone to meet his God, but that man didn't even trust me. He'd make me take my glasses off the minute I'd opened the seal, and I'd have to do the rest of the work just feelin' my way. I'm blind as a mole without my glasses, and that's the way Scotty wanted me. Poor old duck."

"Mr. Miller," said Ames, "do you know whether Scotty knew that Murchison had asked you to take down the readings on the *Hellcat*?"

"Can't say," said Miller. "He kept Buck all tied up talkin' to him while I was busy with the gauge, so it might look, judging it now, that he was helping me. Still and all, knowing Scotty, I'd say if he knew anything about it, he'd have popped off about it after Buck left. So I guess I'd say he didn't know."

Ames rose to go. He shook hands with Miller and said, gravely, "you asked me something a moment ago, Mr. Miller, about keeping what you know quiet. I'll give you a straight answer. Your life probably depends on whether or not you talk."

Ames' lean face, so seldom revelatory of any emotion, was tightly drawn now, and a curious flame burned in his eyes. "What you know can not only clear Buck, Mr. Miller, but it points directly to the man who murdered Scotty. If that gets out, you may need more repairing than you can get in your sheds..." Miller's hand had gone limp by the time Ames let go of it. "You've been a great help," Ames said. "Thanks again."

"Don't mention it," Miller gulped. "I...I...won't."

Walking back to the gyro, Tom observed, dryly, "Ain't

goin' to be much gossip around these parts for awhile."

WHEN they returned to the *arrondo*, one of the hands told Tom that Sue had gone. Lola had returned from Mirabello and taken Sue back with her, to Mirabello City.

"Don't sound like Lola," said Tom. "She'd just as soon take Miss Sue's eyes out before this happened to Buck. I'll take you in, Mr. Ames."

Ames said nothing. It was as if a fever had seized him during that afternoon. He sat quietly in the gyro, his eyes staring fixedly in the distance. But he couldn't keep his hands still. The long, bony fingers wrestled with each other until they were white from pressure. When they were near town, Ames said, "Don't drop me off at Standish. I want to go to the center of town."

Tom skirted Standish port and landed in the small gyro port near the courthouse. "You know where to get me if you need me, Mr. Ames," he said. "I'm right handy in a fight, if I do say so."

Ames walked the two blocks to the offices of the *Twin-Sun*. He went into the circulation room and asked for the files of the last three weeks. A few minutes later, a side door opened and Murchison himself came in, carrying an armful of newspapers.

"How do you do, Mr. Ames?" he said, sitting down beside Ames. He laid the papers down before Ames. "I hope you find these useful."

Ames hesitated a moment before he took the papers. It occurred to him that he might have gone to the library for the back file, but now that he was here, he wasn't sorry. There was no use deluding himself that Murchison didn't know what he was up to—or that he wouldn't have known soon enough if Ames had gone to the library. From here in, Ames thought, the game would be played open-handed.

Picking up the first issue, Ames scrutinized the newspapers until he reached the one dated the 16th. He took out his notebook and copied the caption from under a picture. The picture showed Frank Murchison about to enter a small, private rocketship, the bow of which was emblazoned with two suns. Murchison was waving to the camera.

The caption read: *"Mr. Frank (Bax) Murchison, publisher of the Twin-Sun, as he left this morning for the two-day convention of colonial newspapers, held this year at Church's Planet. Mr. Murchison said, 'Now that the convention has come so close to Mirabello, I am going to see to it that next year's convention is held right in Mirabello!' "*

The issue of the 19th carried another picture of Murchison, taken at the convention. It had been ethergraphed from Church's. Beside it was a speech Murchison had made on the function of the colonial press. Ames kept looking through the succeeding issues carefully, until he had reached the one dated the 26th, where he gave it up.

"You look disappointed, Mr. Ames," said Murchison. "Perhaps I can help you." He had been sitting there close to Ames, watching him.

"As a matter of fact, Mr. Murchison, I am not disappointed. I thought perhaps your paper might have also carried the story of your return from Church's, seeing the interest with which it followed your excursion there."

"Well," Murchison smiled, "my editor thought it would please me. I returned on a poor day, however, the 24th, the night Scotty's ship was found, and the news of the murder seemed more important. Don't you agree?"

Ames shrugged. "I'm afraid I don't understand

newspaper values, Mr. Murchison." He re-stacked the papers, and as he pushed them towards Murchison, for some undefined reason, a wave of uneasiness swept over him. He nodded his goodbye and left.

A few minutes later, across the street from the jailhouse, he went into a phone booth and put in a call to the Wylie *arrando*. He left a message for Tom to call him at home as soon as he reached the *arrando*.

CHAPTER SEVEN

SLOWLY, thoroughly bemused, Ames walked across the street to the jailhouse. A car screeched to a quivering halt two feet from running him down. Ames turned absent eyes in the direction of a series of passionate oaths being hurled at him by the driver. "Sorry," Ames mumbled and walked head-on into a man on the other side of the street.

"Beg pardon," Ames said. "Weather conditions."

The man inquired blankly: "Huh?"

Ames appeared a bit startled. He realized he had uttered the thought *weather conditions* in a distinctly audible voice. "Beg pardon," he apologized, mumbling again, "There's so damned much to remember." It didn't occur to him that he had spoken *that* thought until he was at the jailhouse door. When he turned around he saw the man to whom he had just spoken standing transfixed in the middle of the street. The driver, blocked again, was shouting curses at his new target. Ames smiled the least bit. "Have to stop talking to myself," he resolved, speaking aloud, and went in.

He went down the corridor to the chief turnkey's desk.

That official, hearing him coming, separated from a group of guards and met Ames. He fixed a dour, noncommittal expression on his face.

"Sorry, Mr. Ames," he anticipated. "Can't do a thing about it."

Ames blinked. "Beg pardon?"

"The order came direct from the C.A.," said the turnkey. "I'm here to obey orders. You'll have to talk to him, and if he says no—"

"Would you mind telling me what you're talking about?"

"The order," the turnkey repeated doggedly. He searched Ames' face and seemed to recognize that something was wrong, and before Ames could speak, he said, "The order that you're not allowed to see Buck Wylie." He added, frowning, "Anyway, it's for your own good, the way—"

"What order?" Ames demanded, coming to life suddenly. "What makes Whitley think he can bar a lawyer from seeing his client? Has he taken to writing in new laws?"

"—the way," the turnkey finished, his voice growing perplexed toward the end, "the way Buck said what he'd do to you if he laid his hands on you," and then, in sudden understanding: "Don't you know you ain't Wylie's lawyer no more?"

Ames took a deep breath. "No," he said. "Who said so?"

"Wylie. So did his sister. She and—"

"Sue Wylie told you that?"

"That's what I'm telling you. She was here about two, three hours ago with Miss Morales. Then they left and half an hour later Miss Morales came back with Mr. Farley.

Farley told me he was going to be Wylie's lawyer from now on and to keep you out. A little while after that I got the order from Mr. Whitley, to make it official, I guess..." He hesitated. "I thought you knew, Mr. Ames."

"No," Ames said slowly. "No, I didn't." His face had flushed a deep crimson. Now it turned dark and angry as his eyes. He turned and retraced his steps down the corridor, moving slowly.

He was almost at the door when Lola Morales and Farley came in hurriedly. For a fraction of an instant Farley seemed startled, then he regained his stride and his formal, noncommittal expression. The girl glanced at Ames as if he were transparent. They would have walked right past Ames if he hadn't stepped into their path.

"Miss Morales—"

The girl didn't look at Ames. She started to walk around him. Ames followed her movement, blocking her. She stopped a few inches from Ames and behind her Farley came to a halt. The girl's eyes lifted from the floor and met Ames, their black depths filled with hatred.

"I'm not interested," she said in a soft, deadly voice. "Keep away from me."

Her glance fell again and she brushed by Ames. Farley followed her closely, his expression that of a man lost in his own thoughts. Ames watched them until they disappeared down the corridor, then he started for the door again.

His face felt hot but there was a growing coolness in his mind. By the time he reached the street he was walking quickly, and then he increased his pace as if his legs were trying to keep up with the speed of his thoughts. He walked through town with his long legs flying, unaware of the people staring after his lanky, urgent figure.

DUSK was falling, gathering the little town into a soft gray bag through which a rising wind blew, playing in the treetops. When Ames reached his own street there were already lights in several houses, but he made out the figures of Tom and Sue Wylie sitting on his porch. The sight sent a shiver through him. He tried to tell himself that he had known she would be waiting there, but he knew that he had only hoped and that not until the last moment had he been justified in his inner belief that the girl had not betrayed him.

There was no greeting from either as Ames mounted the stairs. He saw the girl's somber, tear-stained face, her swollen eyes. Tom sat beside her, saying nothing.

Ames leaned against the porch railing. "What happened?" he asked.

At his words the girl broke into tears again and Ames saw that she hadn't spoken because she was holding on. He let her cry until her shoulders were still and then he laid his hand on her arm. Presently she grew calmer. She began to speak very quietly, haltingly at first, her eyes closed.

"Someone spoke to Buck...lied to him...about us. When I visited him today he was furious. He said I...I was keeping you on the case because I...we..." Her voice fell away then resumed: "—we were having an affair. I couldn't talk to him—he wouldn't listen. When I tried to deny it he asked me if it wasn't true that I had spent last night here. I had to admit it but I tried to... He wouldn't listen. He slapped me and threw me out. He wouldn't..." She was crying again.

Ames nodded bitterly. "Yes," he said in a dead voice, then hesitated and left the rest unsaid.

"It's Lola!" Tom spat out suddenly. "She's been tryin' to get rid of you—wants to git lawyer Farley in there."

"She's gotten him," Ames said. "After Sue left she went out and brought Farley back with her. I just met them together again. They wouldn't talk to me."

He sighed deeply and was silent. He struggled to keep his spirit alive while he pondered this new aspect of an already overwhelmingly complex problem. At times it seemed to him his head would burst, but there was light on the horizon and it was growing brighter. If the unknown enemy's moves were complicating matters they were also tracing a pattern for someone who could read it.

"Yes," Ames said quietly. "Lola Morales has a double grip on him. She's not only his alibi but she knows that Buck has been lying all along. It's the only answer that makes sense...the only one..."

Sue Wylie was looking up at Ames. She breathed: "Lying?"

Ames softly pounded his thigh with a loose fist. "Yes," he said. "I'll stake my life that there was some kind of connection between Buck and Scotty Purdom—that they were really partners."

"You don't mean that!" Sue Wylie cried. "You can't believe—"

"I'm not saying—"

She seemed beyond reason. Grief had only magnified her loyalty and obscured it with emotion. She rose quickly. "I know what you're saying! You're repeating the lies, the innuendoes—you're taking out your disappointment—"

"Listen to me, Sue!" Ames said loudly. He gripped her arms as she made a move to leave the porch. He was surprised at the energy with which she fought him, struggling to get out of his grasp. He was further confused

79

because he recognized that he was not entirely opposed to her leaving, to avoid the necessity of unraveling thoughts still so tangled that he was uncertain where they might lead. But he could not let her go like this. He had to—

There were loud, excited voices down the end of the street. He saw doors opening, people coming out of their houses. They were calling to the scattering handful of young boys who had descended on the quiet street to hawk their newspapers. The commotion grew louder, and he made out the gist of what the voices were calling. Almost in a dream he heard that Hank Miller had been murdered. The *Twin-Sun* had reason for its extra edition.

For a moment the girl had been still. Tom too had risen and was standing at the edge of the porch. Then the girl took advantage of Ames' relaxed grip and broke free. She ran down the stairs. Ames made no move to follow her. He nodded to Tom's poised hesitation to follow the girl. "Stay with her, Tom. Let me know what happens."

He watched the two figures running down the street towards the center of confusion, his mind adrift in lightless gloom of evening and his thoughts.

CHAPTER EIGHT

AMES leaned back in his chair and forced himself to nibble at a sandwich, washing it down with draughts of cold, bitter coffee. The light of a single lamp cast disordered shadows in his study, illuminating one side of his drawn, thoughtful face. His desk was piled high with scraps of paper, with scrawls and figures and notes, bound only by pencilled lines leading from one to another, as of a man trying to trace a road through inaccurate and incomplete charts of a difficult land. Under the many sheets lay the two-page extra edition of the *Twin-Sun*.

The story was hasty and lurid. Miller had been found shot to death in his sheds. Whatever evidence had been found of his murderer had not been revealed. The investigation was proceeding.

Ames glanced at his watch. More than an hour had passed since Sue Wylie had run away from him. He picked up his papers again and studied them. Presently he took a new sheet and began writing, copying bits from the papers spread before him, following the arrows and lines from one to another. Half an hour went by in this manner before he rose up. He pocketed the final sheet and destroyed the others, then turned out the lamp and left his house.

He walked toward the center of town. In early evening the quiet, dimly lit streets, the great, aged oaks, reminded him of the little town in Indiana where he had spent his boyhood. The memory was disquieting. The excitement of an hour before had gravitated to the town square where it was, by then, increasing by the moment, fed by the constant arrival of new people.

Ames caught snatches of their talk as he passed through the square but paid no attention to them. Again and again he summed up the myriad details he had written down and there was no room in his mind for any intruding thoughts. To the people in the square he must have looked a dreamwalker for all the purposefulness of his quick, long-legged gait.

On the other side of town he ascended the hill to Judge Averill's house. Before he passed through the iron-grille gates that enclosed the handsome white house he paused at the hedge. The decision had to be enforced; it could no longer be postponed. Yet for several minutes more he stood there, stiff-jawed, pensive. The judge's study was lit and through the curtained windows Ames heard music as somber and filled with misgivings as he himself was. He went through the gates and rang...

Not until Brillov's *Symphony of the Spheres* had concluded did Judge Averill turn to Ames. He had met Ames at the door and quickly and silently taken him back to the study, indicated a chair and resumed his listening. It was the night of the weekly concert from Church's, piped in especially by relay to such small communities as Mirabello. When the last movement, strong and triumphant, had died away, Averill methodically lit a cigar and faced Ames.

"You've decided to trust me, young man?"

Ames nodded and said nothing.

The judge thoughtfully blew out smoke. "Forced to, aren't you?" he asked, almost sadly. "They're moving against you very quickly."

Ames said: "Yes, sir. I've got to do it this way or not at all. If I'm wrong, I'll fail. I must hope I'm right." He waited for Averill to say something and when the silence persisted, he said, "You've heard about Miller, of course?"

"Of course."

Ames said suddenly; "Murchison did it. He had Miller killed just as he either killed Scotty himself or ordered his murder."

Judge Averill kept looking at Ames expressionlessly.

"I can prove these things," Ames said. "I want you to give me the power to prove them."

"How?"

Even-voiced, Ames said, "I want you to confiscate all of Miller's private business records. I want all of Murchison's files and records. I want you to grant me access to the impounded ships, Scotty's and Buck Wylie's."

JUDGE AVERILL contemplated his cigar. He shook his head. "You know I have no right to do what you ask."

"I know. I am hoping that the greater right, the essential justice behind it, will allow you to overlook the minor wrong you may be committing."

"And you believe that if I did what you ask that you could conclusively prove Murchison's guilt?"

Ames met the old jurist's keen eyes. He could not penetrate them. Ames lips thinned. "No," he said. "I can't be sure. I can only hope. I still need facts. Facts, facts..." he leaned forward in his chair, smashing his fist in his palm, his voice intense and low, "...facts like links in a chain around Murchison."

"And if you're wrong?" asked the judge quietly, peering at Ames from under his heavy brows. He waited, then added, "I have lived here a long time, Ames. I have devoted my life to the law—"

"Law!" Ames cried out, getting up swiftly. There was anger in his voice now. He advanced to the desk behind which the judge sat. "I'm getting tired of the law." Ames ground out contemptuously. "What is law in a case like this? What kind of law is it that allows the guilty to use it as a cloak? The law should be impartial—if it can't help the innocent to hell with it. I'll get around it. I'll monkey with it—"

"Yes?"

It wasn't the mildness with which the old man had spoken that stopped Ames short. Rather it was an awareness that his words had taken hold somehow. There was a different look in those wise old eyes. It was gone by the time the judge spoke, but whatever subtle difference had been expressed there now lay, transformed as it were, in his manner. He sounded ironically calm and judicial.

"According to the law none of the things you ask can be done. Why? Because you are not concerned. What protection would an accused man have if anyone was free to tamper with the facts, the details, the fabric of his case? Even as the accused man's lawyer you could not do these things. The law is very clear on such matters—" a cloud of cigar smoke obscured what had been very like a twinkle in his eyes—"as it is on most matters. It has been my experience—and I'm sure you have at some time shared that experience—that it remains clear, although one's view of it may become distorted through various factors."

He sighed, then resumed, "Emotion, for instance," and shook his head. "Or loss of perspective from too great attention to the foreground—the details, you might say, or the—ah—facts. But the law is clear. It says that only the accused, or persons sharing in the accusation, such as material witnesses, may come to the law for the kind of help you want…" He paused. "You understand?"

Ames, tensely attentive, had stood quietly listening to the old man. Judge Averill was saying something to him that was buried in his legalistic manner. It seemed to be emerging.

"But how?" Ames asked presently.

"How?" Averill repeated. He shrugged. "You, the scholar Ames, ask an old backwoods judge how?"

HE DIPPED his cigar gently into an ashtray and began to putter around his desk, glancing at Ames once or twice. Ames' face was flushed, his eyes directed at the floor, his fists clenched. When finally Ames looked up and started for the door, the judge rose and motioned him to wait. The hand that motioned held a thick, gray-covered, paperbound volume. He came up to Ames and showed it to him, though Ames knew what it was.

"The May issue of the Law Review," said Averill quietly. "It just came today." He smiled ruefully. "Not as late as usual. The law moves slowly its wonders to perform." He thumbed through the pages and opened it and held it out to Ames.

Ames took it and started to read: RECENT ENACTMENTS; REGULATIONS; JUDGMENTS: FROM THE INTERPLANETARY COLONIAL COUNCIL. Ames glanced down the index to where, next to GHORT GROUP, a pencil had made a check. He read:

"...and where a crime has been committed and proven to the satisfaction of the state, and where such crime does cause the heirs and assignees of the estate to suffer monetary, property or real losses, or loss of services which heirs and assignees would not, to the satisfaction of the state, have suffered either in the due course of events or had the crime not been committed, then such heirs, assignees, and such parties listed and enumerated under Sec. 4551, Para. 12 of this enactment, shall have recourse to law both for restitution and for penalty judgment, and that all state claims to forfeiture of estate rights as enumerated under Sec. 23 of the Colonial Penal Code, shall be waived and deemed as transferred to such heirs and assignees. Para. 18: All statements, judgments, etc., listed under Para. 17 of the foregoing shall also apply to heirs and assignees of duly contracted partnerships, where such partnerships have been established by law. Para. 19: Sec. 4551 shall be in effect from the date hereinafter inscribed: APRIL 15, midnight, Colonial Central Time. Para. 20: all claims arising..."

Ames looked up and found it difficult to hold the paperbound volume steady. He stared at Judge Averill incredulously. The legalistic rigamarole of the language was astonishingly transparent, involved as it might have been to a layman. For a moment he could not speak, and then a fierce, quiet exultation seized him.

"In other words," he said softly, "if Buck Wylie is convicted of Scotty's murder, then Murchison, as the legal partner of Scotty, not only inherits everything he and Scotty owned—but he can then claim a penalty judgment against everything Buck Wylie owned."

Judge Averill nodded. "Evidently the Council felt the need for an extension of liability laws for the colonies here. There's been some agitation for this kind of thing ever since it was successfully tried in the Spanish Motanga mandate." He was watching Ames as he went on casually. "It reduced the type of premeditated crime common among—"

"But it's the May issue," Ames said, puzzled, "and today is July 28th." He nodded quickly to forestall Averill. "I know it gets here late, but the law itself—that was passed on April 15th." He had become conscious of Averill watching him. "Why didn't you know this before?" Ames asked. "Wasn't it ethergraphed…published…" He broke off.

The beginning of an expression was forming on the judge's face. "The law is clear on that, too. The Council ethergraphs its news laws and regulations to the colonies affected—in this case the entire Ghort Group received it— and it must then be published in every local newspaper."

"I know that. Why do you repeat it?"

"To show you that we *both* know it."

Ames questioned: "And?"

The expression was more evident now. "You won't have to bother checking it," Averill said. "I have already, without fuss, checked it myself. Murchison's *Twin-Sun* never published the new law."

Ames let his breath out with a soft noise.

"Yes," Judge Averill nodded, his face stern and bitter. "When I read this in the Review today, I, too, decided it explained a good deal. It seems to me that Murchison is undoubtedly guilty. But prosecution for not publishing this law would cost him a small fine...where," he nodded again, grimly, "it would appear that true justice calls for a much greater penalty."

IN THE silence Ames worked his hands over his face, rubbing his cheeks until they were red. "Then we both know it," he said. "Conclusive inner knowledge—"

"And no proof."

"No proof!" Ames spat out. But he said no more. His temper, rare to him, hampered his thinking; he was unused to coping with it. He let himself settle to comparative calm, standing there before Averill and saying nothing, but all the while his mind feverish with activity. Then he leaned over the desk, picked up a pencil and a sheet of paper.

"There are two things you can do for me, Judge," he said as he wrote, and added: "Both legal."

"Yes?"

"Send messages for me in Court code to the I. P. and the Bureau of Claims."

"What for?"

"For facts," Ames said. "Facts, facts..." He kept writing for a minute or two more. When he finished he scanned the paper and handed it to Judge Averill.

The judge read what Ames had written and looked at Ames with a bemused, puzzled expression.

"I'll get whatever else I need," Ames said, not offering to explain. "Will you do it?"

"Yes."

"Good. And the rest of it—" Ames grinned horribly— "will be strictly legal, too. Goodnight."

A quarter of an hour later Ames was at a bar in the center of town. He spoke to no one and leaned against the bar, gulping down one drink after another. The buzz of conversation was all around him and he fought off the dizzying effects of the drink and the headache occasioned by the unaccustomed diet and the noise and music. They were still talking about Miller, and, he knew, they were watching him. He stayed at the bar perhaps twenty minutes, then paid for his drinks and walked with only partially feigned unsteadiness to the street and went into another bar on the corner.

Here he repeated the process, drinking a little slower and taken to studying the glasses, occasionally mumbling to himself. He seemed quite drunk by then and he knew he was well noticed. When he called for his fourth drink, the bartender hesitated.

"Think you ought to, Mr. Ames?"

Ames looked up at him, bleary-eyed. "Whazzat?" he demanded, thickly. "Want another drink. Got to have another drink. Make me forget whole damn business, maybe."

The bartender, a kind-faced old man, looked around then leaned over towards Ames. "Maybe you're—" he hesitated, started again. "Don't take offense, Mr. Ames— no offense meant—but maybe you're taking the whole thing too hard."

"Takin' what hard?" Ames asked. "Think I care I was kicked out of my first case? Don't give a damn!" he said belligerently. He grew more confidential in manner but his voice was too loud as he said: "Got to forget somethin' else." He put a finger across his lips. "Shhhh," he said slyly. "I know something could land the whole gang of 'em inna calaboose. Whole gang, especially Murchison. But don't—"

The bartender, aware of the many curious glances now fixed on Ames, tried to stop him. "Now, Mr. Ames—"

"Don't interrupt," Ames said with annoyance, seemingly oblivious of the attention he had attracted from the moment he had entered, and which was now obvious to everyone near him. "I'm not goin' do anything 'bout it. Let 'em all stew. Let Murchison get away—"

"Mr. Ames, please—"

"Am I gonna get my drink or not?" Ames cried, pounding the bar. "No?" He answered his own question and threw a bill on the bar then turned and walked out, declaring loudly: "Go t'nother place where they don't interrupt."

HE HALF staggered out in the street, wandered a few feet down the block, spun around and caught himself before he fell, and seemingly unaware that he had described a circle and was heading back in the direction from which he had come, re-entered the same bar. He walked back to the bartender he had left a few moments before and greeted him with open arms and a fuzzy smile.

"H'lo, Pop!" he declaimed. "Le's have a drink. Just walked out of a bar 'cause wouldn't lemme have a little drink." He put down a crumpled bill, and ignoring the bartender completely, put his arm around a small man who stood at the bar. "Have a drink with me, stranger," he smiled loosely, "and I'll tell you a story'll raise your hair."

He winked. "Got a fine story 'bout Murchison and Buck Wylie and Farley. Got whole thing worked out up here—" He tapped his temple and winced. "Owl No good. Hurts a little." He smiled again, then immediately glowered at the bartender who hadn't moved. "Well? Gonna have trouble with you, too?"

"I'm sorry, Mr. Ames. I can't serve you."

"Why not?" Ames shouted.

The bartender started coming out from behind the bar. Ames saw him coming and backed away uncertainly. A crowd had gathered around him when he came back and now he faced them.

"Fren's and Romans!" Ames cried. "You're all my witnesses. Murchison's arranged to have me kicked out of every bar inn a town because he hates me! And why does he hate me?" he demanded, pointing a long arm at the bartender that kept the old man away effectively. " 'Cause he knows I got somethin' on him—and not only him—" he swept his arm out eloquently, "—but Farley and Wylie too! Got 'em all—"

The bartender had quickly moved in under Ames arm and gripped his long frame. With efficient, practiced movements he began pushing Ames out. There were cries from the crowd to let Ames stay but the bartender took Ames, unresisting but still declaring, to the door. He led him to the street and walked him to the curb.

"Son," he said gently, wheezing a little, "you're going to be a sorry lad in the morning. If you ever had a chance of getting another case in this town, you're losing it tonight. Now why don't you go home and sleep it off?" He shook his head sadly. "You're a good lad. I don't like to see—"

Ames disengaged himself grandly, aware that his audience had followed him to the door. "Unhand me!"

Ames shouted. "I'm going home but I'll be back . Gonna make out papers and sue you for a million! Two million!" And he turned and staggered down the street, singing...

He was a good deal steadier when he walked up the stairs to his house but his face was green and his eyes half closed. He went into the bathroom and stuck a finger down his throat. He retched again and again, then went to the kitchen. He mixed a concoction of egg and milk and tobasco, which he used to wash down two grains of the Mercurian headache patent medicine, *Nixxir*. Finally, alternately belching and sighing, he retired to his study.

He sat for more than hour studying the diagrammatic sheet he had made up earlier that evening and he was asleep on his feet when he wandered wearily to bed. Five minutes later he was back, fumbling with his thick *MacDougal's Interplanetary Torts and Laws*. He thumbed through the pages until he found something that pleased him, then went back to bed.

THERE was a huge bell in the center of Ames brain and someone was beating it with a stone hammer, standing with both feet on Ames eyes. When Ames finally opened his eyes he saw that there wasn't any man and he decided that someone was ringing the bell downstairs. He glanced at his bedside clock, saw it indicated eleven o'clock, and checked on it by opening his eyes wider to see if there was daylight. There was.

He wrapped a robe around his shivering body and went down. He opened the door to admit Sour Tom and let in enough sunlight to warm and blind himself.

"I thought you were dead," Tom said.

"I'd be better off," Ames moaned. "Come in."

He led the way back to the kitchen and immediately

busied himself with making coffee. While he waited for it he took another dose of *Nixxir.* Tom watched him. He hadn't said a word from the moment he had come in.

When Ames felt his voice return he asked: "How is she?"

"Fine," Tom nodded. "Wish I could say the same for you."

"What's the matter?"

"You don't know?"

Ames sighed. "All right."

"What made you do it?"

Ames countered: "What do you think?"

"I ain't sure."

Ames almost smiled. "Then you haven't given me up?"

"Not until I hear you out."

"Thanks," Ames said gratefully. He shook himself, then poured coffee for himself and Tom. He sat down across the small table from Tom and said, "Tell me what you heard. Everything."

Tom sipped his coffee before he spoke: "I heard it all over the place. You went on a binge. Shot your mouth off sayin' you had enough on Wylie and Farley and especially Murchison to hang the lot of 'em." There was a question in his voice the way he said it.

"That's right," said Ames. "What do they think? People, I mean."

"They say you're finished. They don't like to see someone goin' around talkin' mighty because he's been throwed out of a case he didn't have no business bein' in on in the first place."

Ames nodded in obvious satisfaction. He finished his coffee and replenished both cups. Then he said, "Good. Anything else?"

Tom studied him before he answered. There was a new expression in his voice, a new life, as he said, "There's talk that Murchison won't like what you're sayin' about him." After a pause, while Ames drank, he said quietly, "That's the way you want it?"

"Yeah," Ames grinned. "Want to help me?"

"Hank Miller was a good friend of mine."

The name erased Ames' smile. "I'm going drinking again," he said.

"In the middle of the day?"

"Day or night, it's all the same. I've got to keep at it until I get what I'm after. You think I enjoy eating *Nixxir?*"

Tom's forehead creased, "All right," he nodded. "But every other round is on me."

The two men exchanged grins.

AN hour later Ames was telling a wizened little miner: "I'm not jus' standin' here making up stories, I'm givin' you fax. Fax. I know, my friend, I *know.*"

They were in one of the numerous bars that were like weeds in the vicinity of the blastport. At this time of day the bars were deserted, but the few hangers-on there listened to Ames attentively. Tom, in a seeming state of half-stupor, bent an elbow beside Ames and listened too. Like him, Ames appeared to be more than well oiled.

"And what's this you know?" asked the miner, eyes bright with interest.

"Ah," Ames smiled mysteriously. "If I tell you everything I know, you'll know everything you know and everything I know, so you'll know more than me, right? But I got enough on Wylie and ole Murch—" and he winked his incessant, wise wink.

From that bar Ames and Sour Tom wandered to another, a third, a fourth. In each Ames grew more loquacious and provocative, his stories more vague and his hints wilder. By three o'clock, after the arrival of a double shipment of orium and a hired mining crew, his audience was a sizable one. But shortly after three, in the fifth bar, the stories came to an end.

Two men came in to the Idle Hour. One was a head taller than the other, but both were broad and muscular and both wore gun belts slung low from their hips to supplement their deputy's shields. The smaller of the two walked directly up to Ames and touched his arm.

"Your name Terwilliger Ames?"

Ames looked up startled. "Yeah," he admitted belligerently.

"You're under arrest."

"What?" Ames exploded. He stood up to his full height and towered over the short deputy. "Me? Whaffor?" Suddenly he looked crafty. "Got a warrant?" he demanded. "Lessee the warrant!"

The deputy fished out a stiff, folded paper and waved it under Ames nose. "Straight from Judge Averill, signed and sealed, and you're goin' to be delivered. You better come without no trouble."

Surprisingly enough, Ames made no trouble. He submitted meekly and went out to where a large vehicle with wired windows awaited him. If anyone had intercepted the satisfied smile that Ames darted at Tom, it would have surprised them even more. As it was, Tom waved a forlorn farewell and drifted out of the bar.

Everything was ready when Ames was brought in to the courthouse, even to the expectant crowd that greeted his arrival outside. Judge Averill was on the bench, locked in consultation with Farley. Murchison, his face stiff with righteous anger, watched Ames walk up to the bench. Whitley, the Colonial Attorney, came out of a side office. Most of the courtroom was empty—attendants were posted at the doors—but there were more than a dozen men in the first two rows. Ames recognized some of them as having formed part of his audiences the night before and that afternoon.

He hardly listened to the C.A.'s short address to the Court, in which he presented the State's plea. He paid less attention to the men Whitley summoned, one after another, to testify to what they had heard Ames say, a procession halted by Judge Averill after the fourth witness. Farley's speech, in which he alternately pleaded for his client, Buck, and for himself, was by far the most interesting.

Thickly larded with sarcasm, Farley's speech ended, "...and if indeed this drunken oracle knows anything pertaining to this case, then on behalf of my client I feel it is my duty to have Mr. Ames incarcerated and held as a material witness until such time as he can testify under oath before this Court."

Judge Averill nodded. "The Court agrees with the Colonial Attorney and Mr. Farley and finds evidence sufficient to warrant proposed action. However," and he scratched his chin meditatively, "may I ask you, Mr. Farley, whether you believe Mr. Ames actually has any testimony worthy of this Court's consideration?"

Farley sneered. "I view his remarks with the utmost contempt."

"The Court agrees with you, Mr. Farley. Motion to hold defendant as material witness granted." The judge made a notation on some of the papers spread before him, then looked up. "However, in view of counsel's opinion of the defendant's worth as a witness, the Court holds him in bail of five dollars and cautions—"

"Five dollars!" Murchison burst out wrathfully. "Why, that's—"

JUDGE AVERILL rapped his gavel once. "—and cautions him to silence on pain of being arraigned for contempt of court."

Farley, scarcely able to contain himself, gulped: "If it please the Court, counsel submits that Mr. Ames' further liberty might prejudice my client's case beyond repair—"

"The Court has already cautioned him, Mr. Farley."

"But, your Honor, he has already said enough."

"The Court has entered him as a material witness."

"Your Honor, his innuendoes concerning Mr. Murchison and myself certainly merit some protection from this Court."

"Are you proposing a separate action, Mr. Farley?"

"If it please the Court, yes."

Judge Averill thought a moment, then said: "Decision reserved."

Farley's face had long since turned crimson. Now it threatened to become violet. "But, your Honor," he spluttered, "a bail of five dollars—*five dollars*—is hardly…hardly…"

The judge leaned over and surveyed Farley with impartial curiosity. "Come, come, Mr. Farley. You said yourself you had contempt for his value as witness. Surely you don't consider five dollars too high an estimate of your contempt?"

Farley tried to gather himself together. He glanced at Whitley, who stood by rigidly, and at Murchison, whose face was queerly blown up. His lips worked a little and he seemed to be undergoing some internal process that pained him. A new light was beginning to show in his eyes; it shone through his bewilderment. For a moment he seemed on the verge of plunging ahead but he stopped, looking from the judge to Ames. In his stead, C.A. Whitley came forward, officious and flustered.

"Your Honor, the State moves to increase bail to fifty thousand dollars." He paled before Averill's sharp scrutiny. "The State bases its claim on Mr. Ames' reputation."

"Mr. Ames' reputation is well known to the Court," said Averill, slowly. "Petition denied. This Court stands adjourned." He rose from the bench and motioned to Ames. "Mr. Ames, I want to see you in my chambers, if you please."

Ames nodded respectfully and waited until the judge had left the courtroom. He took in the silent consternation Averill had left behind him. Whitley and Farley and Murchison were still regarding Ames, as if they expected their combined examination would yield the answer. With no expression, Ames picked his path through them and followed Averill.

The judge was leaning against a desk. He had taken off his robes and was in the act of choosing a cigar from a case on the desk when Ames came in. He glanced at Ames and rolled the cigar in his fingers. "You're a remarkable young man, Ames," he said dryly, pleased.

"Thank you, sir. You understood, of course?"

"Of course I understood."

"But, but—" Ames fumbled uncertainly, "you're worried?"

"Yes, I am," said Averill. He lit the cigar, regarded it.

"I'm worried about what they may do. We didn't fool them, you know."

Ames nodded. "I never hoped to be able to fool them. I'm playing my hand open—so open that it would take—"

Averill interrupted impatiently. "You still hold to your thesis that Murchison won't use force? That he will play your game, matching wits?" He sniffed at the expression on Ames' face. "Surprised that I'm aware of your strategy, young man? Come now, it's obvious enough. You succeeded in getting yourself held as a material witness, but you went about it in an astonishingly direct way. Why shouldn't you have assumed Murchison would shut you up with a bullet? Why assume he would go to the trouble of having you arraigned?"

"But didn't you think of that last night?" Ames countered. "I take little credit for my success in your Court, sir. You practically told me exactly what to do."

"I'm reconsidering, Ames. I didn't like the way they looked at you out there. I think. Murchison is growing tired of the game. It's becoming too dangerous for him. He's the kind of gambler who doesn't enjoy the game unless the dice are his."

Ames looked perplexed. "Granted, then. I assume he will use force, sooner or later, but only when he's sure he's lost. What would you advise me to do? Quit?"

"Why not?"

"Why not?" Ames echoed. "What about that little talk on justice I enjoyed so much? What about your telling me—"

"Words, words," said Averill. "Your life's at stake, Ames. It's a big stake to gamble with."

Ames said slowly: "I won't quit."

THE judge nodded, inhaled and blew out a thick cloud of smoke. He allowed a smile to grow on his face until its warmth had changed him completely from the man he had seemed a moment before. He went to Ames and put a hand on his shoulder.

"I'm glad," he said soberly. "I didn't want you to think that perhaps I was pushing you into something you didn't fully understand. It's been a game until now, but that's over with. Sooner or later, as you say, you'll have to stop being a clever lawyer long enough to slug it out—isn't that the expression? —with them. As long as you know it, I'm not afraid for you."

He returned to the desk and picked up several papers. "I've had these for several hours," he said, offering them to Ames. "I think they answer your questions rather fully."

Ames hastily took the official maroon sheets. They were answers from the I. P. and the Bureau of Claims. Above the jumbled letters of their code the judge had carefully lettered a translation of each.

The I. P. message read:

FROM: I.P. REGIONAL HQ. 41ST GRP. CHURCH'S PLANET. 7-29

TO: REGIONAL MAGIS. B.P. AVERILL. MIRABELLO CITY.

RE: INQUIRY VIZ F. MURCHISON, MIRABELLO CITY AND/OR PARTIES CONNECTED WITH IIURABELLO CITY TWIN SUN DATED 7-28

ADVISE F. MURCHISON, PUBLISHER OF MIRABELLO CITY TWIN-SUN MADE INQUIRIES AT CENTRAL I.P. HQ. MARCH 8 CONCERNING CRIMINAL RECORD BRUCE (BUCK) WYLIE. FULL INFORMATION AND DATA FURNISHED

MURCHISON ON MARCH 11. AUTHORITY ICC, PUBLIC SERVICE REGULATION, SEC. 122.

The message from the Bureau of Claims read:

FROM: CLAIMBUR, ICC HQ. COMMERCE DIV. URANIAN SEC. 7-29

TO: REGIONAL MAGIS. B.P. AVERILL. MIRABELLO CITY

RE: INQUIRY VIZ BRUCE (BUCK) WYLIE, SCOTT PURDOM JOINT OWNERSHIP FILES, NEW CLAIM DIVISION, COVERING ONE YEAR, FROM 7-28

THIS PAST FEB. 5 JOINT CLAIM ENTERED BY BRUCE WYLIE AND SCOTT PURDOM IN FULL AND EQUAL PARTNERSHIP, LEGALLY ENTERED, SEALED AND SWORN BY PROXIES HERE: HAYES AND HAYES, ATTORNEYS. SECRET CLAUSE INVOKED BY BOTH. LOCATION CANNOT BE PUBLISHED UNTIL AUG. 5 UNDER AUTHORITY ICC CLAIMS REG. SEC. 42, ALLOWING SIX MONTHS' PRIVATE EXPLOITATION.

WARNING: THIS COMMUNICATION SECRET UNLESS LEGAL EXCEPTION GRANTED OR UNDERTAKEN BY COMPETENT AUTHORITY, ICC PENAL CODE, SEC. 370. FOR PREMATURE PUBLICATION RIGHTS APPLY ABOVE.

Ames carefully folded both sheets and returned them to Averill. His face was flushed and eager. He kept his voice restrained with some difficulty.

"That does it," he said. "It proves two things I suspected. It tells me that Murchison knew about Buck

Wylie's past as far back as March 11th but kept it to himself for four months. More important, it confirms my idea that Buck and Scotty were partners and have been since February 5th." He paused. "What's this about a secret clause and six months of private exploitation?"

"It's a protective measure usually invoked when miners stake out a new claim. If they had to publish the whereabouts of their claim immediately, it would produce a staking rush. This gives them a chance to get set up properly before the territory is swamped."

"I see. Is six months the maximum secrecy allowed?"

"Since Section 42 was passed five years ago."

"And before that? I mean, how is it Scotty Purdom was allowed to keep his Silver Spoon a secret claim for so many years?"

"You see what happened to Scotty. That's why the law was passed; secrecy invited assassination too often— exactly what Wylie is being charged with. Naturally, however, all claims filed before the law was passed do not come under its jurisdiction except by voluntary petition, which Scotty avoided like a plague."

Ames nodded thoughtfully.

Judge Averill picked up the other sheets he had taken and handed them to Ames.

"You wanted these?"

Ames took the papers and read them quickly. They were court orders addressed specifically to one Sam Kaine, Colonial Sheriff in Rheykavike, a smaller city several hundred miles from Mirabello City. There were three of them; one for the seizure and examination of Hank Miller's records, one for Murchison's private files and effects, one allowing Ames access and examination of the impounded *Spoon Special* and *Hellcat*. The petitioner for these rights was listed as Terwilliger Ames, material witness in the case of State vs. Wylie.

Ames picked up a pen and added a notation including the impounding and examination of Buck Wylie's *Gaucho*. He showed it to the judge and handed him the pen. Averill signed underneath. He watched Ames pocket the papers.

"Ames," he said quietly, "I don't really know what you're doing. I have a great respect for you, but I think you still have one valuable lesson to learn—that somewhere you must stop working with paper and start working with human beings. It's quite a different thing." He hesitated, then added: "I do know this—the instant you put this authority into action, you serve notice on Murchison that you're in this to the end. Good luck."

Ames took the proffered hand. "I'm glad you didn't add goodbye," he said, and grinned.

CHAPTER NINE

IT WAS several minutes past midnight when the two official cars sped up to the *Twin-Sun* building and ground to a halt. Colonial Sheriff Kaine, Ames and three deputies got out of the first car. From the second four more men alighted, two of whom stayed behind outside while the rest swiftly entered the building. Downstairs the presses were rolling with noisy thunder.

The men moved with sureness, answering no questions after Kaine served the managing editor with the court order. They entered Murchison's private office and emptied the files. Other deputies confiscated a duplicate file of the *Twin-Sun*. One of Kaine's men, a bony-fingered, thin fellow, worked on Murchison's safe until it opened under his smooth touch. Ames and Kaine stood by, checking everything taken. The raid had been carefully planned.

The phone jangled and Kaine picked it up.

"Sheriff Kaine speaking." His face tightened. "Sorry, Murchison; court order...Averill...Today...Yes... Yes... You were served, weren't you? ...That's your funeral."

He replaced the phone and continued with his checking.

Ames asked, "Your men have trouble at Murchison's home?"

"Some. He refused to open his safe. They threatened to blast."

Fifteen minutes later when they were ready to leave, Kaine picked up the phone, spoke into it. He waited, cursing—Ames caught a reference to his distaste for the hopelessly antiquated telephone on hopelessly antiquated Mirabello—then spoke his name. He listened a moment and hung up. To Ames he said, "It went all right at Miller's. They'll bring his papers in soon. Nobody tried to interfere."

At Standish Port, Sour Tom was waiting. He had come in from the Wylie *arrando* where deputies had cracked the *Gaucho's* Berry gauge with official keys and copied her listings. Tom had brought a copy, which he gave to Kaine. The party took the official gyro and left the blastport. It was just past one.

By three o'clock they were in the government sheds near Mayville. The large, shadowed forms of the *Spoon Special* and the *Hellcat* rested side by side on their vehicular launching blocks, two ships of seven or eight impounded by the government for one reason or another. The great sheds with their lofty, arching roofs were dark and filled with vast echoes and the men who moved on the stone floors seemed like so many preoccupied ants.

They had trained great lights on both vessels. Inside each two-man teams of specialists worked on the Berry gauges with their nitro keys. The work was tedious and painstaking, and every bit of it was carefully and officially photographed on a continuous film. When the gauges were removed, their listings were slowly unwound before the cameras as part of the record. Other men stood by copying the listings and by the time the raw film was sealed in cans, the operations complete, these men had delivered their copies to Sheriff Kaine.

From there Ames retired to a government office. Kaine and several clerks were with him, working through the night. Papers filled with calculations spread over desks and voices spoke quietly, comparing figures as they were passed to Ames. The hours passed and the shaded lights paled before the oncoming dawn, and still Ames worked on tirelessly, his voice rising now and again above the others to demand a repetition. He seldom sat down, pacing the room with long streamers of papers in his hands, his brow furrowed. He fought off fatigue until his eyes were red-streaked slits in a mask of weariness.

Once Kaine stopped him. He had a flask of whiskey and a paper cup. "Better ease up, Ames," he yawned. "You look dead. Have a shot."

Ames shook his head. "Never touch the stuff," he said.

Sheriff Kaine, in the act of yawning, almost choked. His mouth sagged and he stared at Ames. It wasn't until a minute or so later, when Ames realized that the sheriff had undoubtedly heard of his two enormous drinking bouts, that he laughed at the sheriff's expression. Then he sat down on one of the desks and rested long enough to drink some of the coffee Tom had brought in for everyone…

EVEN the drawn blinds were finally ineffective against the sun. The night's vigil showed in the worn faces of the men around Ames. He himself was finally running down. His head was a spinning mass of bits of information, shooting live sparks—dates, ratios, and mileages—through his body. At half-past eight he gave up. He sat down.

"Finished?" Kaine asked when one of his men roused him.

Ames shook his head. "No. I left a lot of my notes at home and I can't go on without them. But I'm through here. I can't thank you enough, Sheriff."

Kaine smiled sleepily. "If I can go home now, that's thanks enough. I'll see that everything's filed according to the book."

And so it was that Ames and Sour Tom were escorted to the gyro that had brought them to Mayville and took off for Mirabello City. When Ames got home and walked down the dusty road to his house, he leaned on Tom, unable to keep his eyes open. Tom kept shaking him, imploring him to walk straight.

"For your own sake," he pleaded. "These neighbors of yours keep seein' you stagger around day after day and your reputation ain't goin'—"

He stopped speaking in silent wonder. He had never heard a walking man snore. And Ames was snoring, deep and rhythmically, as he stumbled on. "I seen everything now," Tom whispered to himself. He took Ames in, undressed him, and put him to bed. Then he sat down to sleep in a chair.

When Tom woke he found the bed empty. He started to jump from the chair and was stopped by two things;

first, his cramped, aching joints, and second, the reassuring sound of Ames pacing downstairs. He became conscious of the ternal smell of strong coffee, this time mixed with burning food. A glance through the shutters told him the day had become late afternoon.

He went downstairs quietly and passed by the door to Ames' study without being noticed. In the kitchen a griddle had long since melted and burned cheese and toast, and whatever coffee had been in the old-fashioned dripolater had disappeared in clouds of vapor. He busied himself with new sandwiches and coffee. Now and again he heard Ames talking out loud to himself.

At length he brought in a tray to the study. Ames heard him come in, nodded absently and appreciatively, and continued pacing. Tom sat down and bit into one of the sandwiches loudly and sipped his coffee with noisy relish. Ames progressed from inattentiveness to frowning to looking at Tom and ended by sighing. He stopped walking in front of the tray and picked up a sandwich. He took a bite and sat down, eating voraciously until he had cleaned the tray. When he replenished his cup of coffee he took notice of Tom again.

"I've got it worked out," he said. "It doesn't make sense now, but it will because it must."

Tom grunted. "What must?"

"The Hive."

"What above the Hive?"

Coffee in hand, Ames unfurled a large chart on his desk. It was an official mariner's chart of the Forty-First System Group. There were numerous red and blue pencilled lines and markings, with figures and notations liberally sprinkled in the empty areas. Ames began to talk in a low, eager voice about navigation, weather reports, gauge markings, mileages, asteroid belts, vacuum impact and other matters. His fingers kept tracing lines along the chart, and no matter where they started, they always ended in a small area in the upper left of the chart. From the moment Ames first indicated that area, Tom never took his eyes off it, his attention firmly riveted. When finally he spoke, his face seemed older and more deeply lined.

"What're you aimin' to do?" he asked slowly, interrupting.

"It's plain enough, isn't it?"

"I ain't heard more'n half of what you said. All I hear is you sayin' things about the Hive. There's no use talkin' about the Hive."

Ames stopped short. "No?"

"No." Tom gestured with a hand. "You can git there easy enough with a finger on a chart. Goin' there yourself—" He broke off and fixed Ames with his eyes. "Or am I makin' a mistake?" he asked.

"You're tight," said Ames. "I'm going to the Hive."

Tom didn't bother answering. He just frowned a little and shook his head and remained silent. He was breathing audibly now, troubled.

"Don't you see?" Ames said. "Every calculation, every—"

"I don't see," Tom cut in. "Suppose you figgered out that you had to go to Kingdom Come for an interview with poor Hank Miller. You think wantin' to go bad enough could make it possible—that and comin' back too?" he added.

"I didn't say I wanted to enter it," Ames said. He waited until Tom's heavy, sad smile faded. "I just want to get close to it."

"How close?"

"That depends."

"On what?"

"On lots of things."

Tom nodded. "Things like those mileages you been figgerin'. How come all these diagrams of yours end right in the Hive, not just close?"

Ames shrugged and made no answer. He contemplated his chart with a distant air. "You can't talk me out of it, Tom," he said presently. "You can make it tougher for me this way, but I'm going."

Tom regarded him. "Got a ship? Know how to navigate?"

Ames remained lost in thought, then silently began to gather his notes and charts. "I'm going," he said quietly. He continued putting his things together and packed them in a small bag. Then he took out the Foster IV pistol, examined its chambers and stuck it in his belt under his loose coat. His lean, earnest face was calm. He was wondering where he—

"Tell you somethin'," Tom interrupted his thoughts. "I really believe you're goin' to go there, one way or another. Any man's damn fool enough to do that needs a body to look out for him. Guess I'm it."

Ames turned sideways to look at him. Their grins met.

THE *Rainbow* was aptly named, if not for her past glories then for the bright streaks of rust and corrosion and decay that covered her hull. She had once been a privately owned yacht, then an auxiliary vessel for Airways, Ltd. and in the twilight of her career she had been a sort of bus for a mining company, transporting men and materials for small distances. She had, within the last year, made perhaps two short hauls, the more recent of these three months before.

She was ancient and cumbersome and far from pretty, but she was space worthy and the only vessel Ames and Tom could lay their hands on quickly, so they hired her. Or rather, Ames had hired her. He listened to Tom's objections—the rental was more than she would have brought in an outright sale…if they waited a day or two, Tom might swing a deal with a friend of his…in any case, if they seemed less anxious and waited—but Ames asked only one question: *Could she make the trip?* And when Tom reluctantly agreed that she probably could, Ames took her.

The preparations—fueling, blastpapers, navigation permit, clearance, shipping order—took time. It was two o'clock in the morning when the *Rainbow* was ready in her pit, her stubby nose pointed to the sky. The word had gone round and her departure was not unattended. The story of the preceding night's raids had added to the speculation, and when the Standish port lights switched on, they disclosed clusters of sky-faring men gathered around in a loose circle. Inside the *Rainbow* Tom had settled at the controls, waiting for the tower's blast signal. Ames, a quiet, worn expression on his face, sat beside him.

A white light flashed in the tower. Tom's hand moved and the ship shuddered as her aft tubes exploded. The dark pit became a well of purple and orange light. The tubes went on and off in rotation, the aft port and starboard, the thwartships, the bow, the auxiliaries, the emergency, and then back to the stern. The aft tubes began to roar more loudly and the ship shivered in every strake.

The tower flashed three greens. "Givin' way," Tom murmured, and his fingers played on the control board. The *Rainbow* exploded with a short series of aft blasts that swiftly blended. As if gathering herself for the leap, the ship steadied. There was a single flash of light, a violet streak shot through with brilliant copper, and the *Rainbow* was rocket-borne. She bit into the sky like a thing alive.

Moments later, Tom turned to Ames. "She likes being up here," he sighed. "She's a good old girl. Maybe she's got memories."

An hour later, with the vessel fixed on course, Tom switched in her gyro pilot and went to sleep. Ames had dropped off almost at the start. He lay tilted back in his seat like a drugged man. Whatever misgivings he had had, whatever troubled visions had flitted through his mind, he knew that at last he had committed himself. There was no turning back now, no matter what the outcome.

With the coming of morning, the golden twin-sunned morning of their little corner of the universe, Ames was in the galley. They ate and spoke of minor matters. Ames remembered little things that had happened to him that amused Tom and the older man was full of anecdotes of the region. Once they spoke of Sue Wylie. Tom had seen her briefly. She was staying with a friend. She had kept trying to see her brother, even begging Farley to intercede for her. It had been useless. Ames knew the feeling. When he thought of her something interfered with his breathing. He had to busy himself...

THIRTY-TWO hours out, the *Rainbow* raised the outlying bodies of the asteroid belt. Green and gray the islands lay in the sky, like stepping stones toward a boundless horizon. The ship slid in past their invisible periphery and slackened speed a bit. Another hour passed and the belt grew thicker, the asteroids appearing in slow-moving groups. It was becoming ticklish to maneuver the *Rainbow* and her speed was dropping off little by little.

Ames stared at the ship's Berry gauge, now and again copying her reading and rapidly working out his calculations. Once Tom, after cutting off a pair of tubes, asked: "How much further?" and Ames shrugged.

"Not much, I think," Ames said, but when he glanced up at Tom's face, he knew the answer was inadequate. He pointed to the notes that lay on the outspread chart in his lap. "I'll try to explain it, Tom," he went on. His fingers traced patterns as he spoke.

"I've got the Berry readings from three ships—the *Spoon Special* of Scotty's, and Wylie's *Hellcat* and *Gaucho*. I've worked them all out to powers of four hundred, to simplify them, and to eliminate small discrepancies that would be natural in comparing high numbers."

"I don't get it," Tom said.

"It's like this, we know that Scotty took both the *Special* and the *Hellcat* with him. So the readings of both should be more or less the same. They won't be exactly the same for various factors—for instance, Scotty took Wylie back to Mirabello in the *Special* and then returned to the *Hellcat*, which he had space-anchored some fifty miles out, so there's a discrepancy of at least a hundred miles already. Again, the *Special* was found wandering in circles on the twenty-fourth, the day it was found. No one knows how long it wandered, so there'd be another discrepancy there. But the distances both ships traveled are great enough not to allow minor differences—a few hundred or thousand miles—to interfere if you work in large powers. All right?"

"Sounds all right."

"It is. It works. Taking the last twenty readings for the three ships shows interesting results. Buck says that he helped Scotty tow the *Hellcat* out fifty miles, then Scotty took him back, and the next day he left on a prospecting trip. He says he has a witness that he came back with Scotty, but supposing he hasn't, what then? The prosecution—"

"What d'you mean, no witness?"

"I won't go into that now. Let's take the prosecution's case. It hasn't given out its version of the crime yet, but it has two alternatives. If Buck has no witness, it can claim he never came back. It can say he went along with Scotty in the *Hellcat*, behind the *Special*, and he then killed Scotty and brought both ships back." He held up a hand to keep Tom from interrupting. "Or, if Buck produces a witness, it can claim he knew where Scotty was going and followed him there the next day. He then killed Scotty and brought both ships back—"

"Nuts!" Tom ejaculated. His eyes were on their course. The asteroids were thicker; two points off the starboard bow there was a large group moving toward them slowly. "You can't tell me that Scotty would take Buck along to his secret mine, or that the prosecution would claim anything so stupid. Nobody'd swaller that. And the same goes for Buck knowin' where to foller him."

"I didn't say Scotty went to his secret Silver Spoon. The prosecution said that, but it knows as well as you and I know that it could hardly—" He stopped. "Look, Tom, I'm not trying the case now. I don't want to go into it. Take my word for it that they have their case, and that they can switch it beautifully when the time comes."

"Meanin'?"

"Suppose they claim that Buck knew exactly where Scotty was going because Scotty was going to a mine they held in partnership?"

Bitterly, Tom said: "That the best you can do? Nuts again."

"The fact is," Ames said gently, "that there is proof they were partners in a new claim." He waited until Tom slowly turned his head toward him. "It's true," Ames nodded. "They'll be able to prove it shortly. However, I'm not saying they'll claim that. It's just one of the possibilities I'm ready for. But let's go back to this…"

HE HELD up a sheet with three columns of figures. "Here is a comparison of the readings on the three ships. I've got them written from the twentieth to the twelfth, but you don't have to study them beyond the fifteenth—the preceding fourteen are completely divergent, just as the *Gaucho's* readings are entirely different all the way through."

Tom studied the sheet. It read:

SPOON		
SPECIAL	HELLCAT	GAUCHO
(20) .9	.4	1.4
(19) 76.2	76.2	288.1
(18) .3	.3	112.2
(17) .3	.3	99.2
(16) 76.5	76.5	166.7
(15) .7	.2	343.3
(14) 4.6	81.4	8,054.6
(13) 19.4	7.1	655.1
(12) 18.3	322.6	181.9

"Okay," Tom said, presently, handing it back. "But you remember what I told you about it bein' easy to fake them readin's?"

"Exactly. Offhand, no one would claim that the *Gaucho* had been where the *Special* and *Hellcat* had been, from these readings. It goes further than that. First, nowhere does the *Gaucho's* readings—and I have them much further back—resemble any of the figures on these two. Second, even assuming it was still possible to fake, nowhere is there a reading for point three—something that shows up twice in succession on both the *Special* and the *Hellcat*. So, from the almost exact similarity in the readings of two of these ships, I assume they went to—together and in the duplication of that point three reading, I look for the crux of the matter.

"Suppose we start with 15. It reads .2 for the *Hellcat*, and that is a root symbol for fifty miles, according to my calculations. Fifty miles agrees with Buck's story: he said Scotty anchored the *Hellcat* fifty miles out and then went back in the *Special*. That gives the *Special* two extra trips of approximately that distance. At 15, the *Special* reads .7 which is close enough. At 16, both ships traveled the same distance to some objective. They went 76.5, stopped, went 3, stopped again, went .3 and then 76.2 again.

"From this I would say that they concluded the trip there after the first .3. The second was recorded on the return trip, which is shown again by the duplication of the 76-odd figure. Both then stopped, and the *Hellcat* came in. But the *Special* kept going round and round, as she was seen—which explains why the last recording for the *Special* is .9 compared to the *Hellcat's* .4 —in other words, the extra .5 involved may be assumed to have been spent circling. Do you see it now?"

"I'm not sure," Tom said slowly. "According to your figures, where are we now?"

Ames took down the Berry reading, worked a few moments, then said softly, "At 74.1. We're getting close."

Tom looked out of the bow. The *Rainbow* was crawling along at half-speed. The sky was studded with asteroid islands. They swung in their unknown orbits on every side.

"Close to what?" Tom asked quietly. "We're gettin' mighty close to the Hive itself."

"I know," Ames nodded.

Tom looked at him. "There's lots you haven't explained. For instance, you could leave Standish port and travel your 76 distance in any direction—along at least hundreds of lines. What made you decide on this bearing?

Ames shook his head. "There's a complicated answer to that one, I'm afraid," he said, almost smiling. "Let it wait. I may be wrong," he added, and when he looked out, the half-smile vanished.

But Tom was unsatisfied. Irritable and curious he asked, "And where in blazes can a jump like that little point three take you out here?" and he swung an open palm in a bewildered, questioning arc.

Ames kept scanning the horizon. "I don't know, I don't know. It is a little jump, isn't it?" He shook his head again. There was no use looking for the answer yet. That would come when it came. By the very nature of its strangeness it would compel attention to itself, in due time. In due time...

The phrase kept repeating itself in his mind. When would that time come? Would it be a matter of a split second—would the failure to notice it become a perilous mission?

For the *Rainbow*, moving ever more slowly, was in a dangerous world now. It was a world filled with moving shapes, with smaller and stranger worlds. Above below the little ship, and in every direction, the sky was filled with forms that gyrated in increasing speed as the ship slowed.

CHAPTER TEN

AMES looked at many of them through the navigator's glass. How still they were. There was no life on them. Some were bare, dead worlds of dust and gray moss, with the rotting hulks of strange trees standing stiff and gaunt. Some were beds of lava, thick sluggish balls of brown and red-streaked mud that burst into viscous, creamy bubbles as the surface exploded from the asteroid's fiery heart. Some were perfect little worlds, greening, fresh, alive, delightful miniatures like a child's vision of Paradise, waiting only for the innocent foot of exploration to give itself to a claimant.

The silence of these silent worlds had invaded the ship. The two men sat in the bow, saying nothing, one preoccupied with the management of the vessel, the other with his thoughts, and with the wonder of where the ship had come. How swift these forms were in their flight as they moved one with another in an intricate dance through the sky... He knew they had come to it even before Tom spoke...

"The Hive." The two words fell dry from Tom's tight lips.

Yes, this, must be the Hive. It was still a few points dead ahead. It was a place where the worlds were almost infinitely more numerous and tightly packed. They were smaller worlds, some of them hardly a few acres, round and swift. Together their gigantic, swirling mass was too great for the eye or the navigator's glass to encompass, and singly they were nothing. They moved around each other in bewildering, erratic patterns, kept in their course by some strange compulsion that alone understood their being. It was as if some giant, compounded of a force beyond man to understand, had tossed a giant's handful of spheres into the sky, and there they had remained, kept tossing and turning and revolving by the undiminished impetus of the Force, locked in orbits forever. Sometimes they brushed by one another so closely that their flowers—when it happened to two living worlds—could have exchanged pollen. Sometimes they came hurtling through space toward each other as if intent at mutual destruction, only to be caught and swerved aside at the last moment, and they would part and swim from view, lost in the vast sky, in the twilight vastness of distance and followed by more.

But they were so close together, their approaches so sudden and incalculable, that the spaces between them could not be entered into. A brown sphere would emerge from the mass, dance along the edge a little and abruptly be sucked into the whirling vortex. A group would separate from the mass, rotate outside wildly, then break apart and disappear at oddly spaced intervals to rejoin the Hive in a new pattern. The pattern changed from instant to instant. There was no sense there, no meaning...

Ames put his pencil down finally. The Berry gauge had read 76.1 and the *Rainbow* had come to a halt. She lay in the sky near the Hive, an idle, rust-streaked speck. In the silence it seemed to Ames he could hear music remarkably like the *Symphony of the Spheres*. It was a weird succession of harmonies, deep and troubled at times, slow moving and majestic, and then rising quickly to lyrical heights until the body of the music was all but gone and all that remained were great masses of strings being plucked in an evasive, exhilarating melody. Then reeds would echo wildly and the sky break into blue, white-flaked streamers of light and the drums would rumble. Then quiet again.

THERE was something wild and ghostly in the sky, something that penetrated the beings of the two men. When Tom spoke again, after an interminable silence, his voice was low and unsteady.

"We can't go any further."

"Then we'll stay here."

"Here?" Silence again. "For how long?"

"I don't know." Ames' eyes met Tom's. He felt it difficult to speak and yet there was comfort in speaking. It was as if uttering words helped to order his thoughts, the way moments of stress would make him talk aloud to himself. "We'll wait here until it makes sense. Everything else has led me here, a hundred little answers combining to form this one question: where from here? But there must be an answer, and we'll wait here until we know it...or until," and he looked out again, somber and thoughtful, "we know that we'll never know any more. Now you go to sleep. I'll sit here and keep looking."

He had no way of knowing when it was that Tom had fallen asleep, but after awhile he knew that Tom had dropped off. From then on there was hardly any time or awareness of it. There was only this incredible small universe and the music of its existence, the law that was itself, the mystery of its being, the unfathomable reasons for the comings and goings of the tiny worlds that composed it. Hours drifted by.

Then Tom was awake and they spoke now and then and again there would be silence between them as they listened. Perhaps he had dozed off himself—it seemed sometimes as if Tom had been asleep and awake half a dozen times—and twice they had eaten, content to nibble at the emergency rations, to drink the vacuumed cold water. Ames felt that his eyes were heavy in their sockets and the pain of keeping them open was a fiery ache that numbed his brain. And hours ran together.

What was he searching for? What had he expected to find here? Had his myriad of, foolish, unimportant little answers arrayed themselves from some malicious, inner intelligence to lead him to a vast and mocking question? Was there some basic antagonism among facts for men who used them? Were they alive and did they resent their captivity? Had there been a time—long before man, long before an inquisitive intelligence lived—when there were no facts as such, and only the immutable mysteries of creation, content to be, to remain?

He was thinking nonsense now, he knew. He was tired, so tired. Facts, facts, facts…like the plucking of strings. What strange things the tired mind was capable of thinking. What were facts? Compact, tiny bundles that tiny intelligences had grasped and formed and fashioned into tools? What could the intelligence do, confronted by this? How could it comfort itself?

"Tom!" Ames whispered loudly.

"Huh?" He had been awake then. He grunted, his voice uncertain and anxious, his eyes turned reluctantly to Ames.

"Tom! Watch that small body there—the red one, with the red moss and water! Watch it come out of the pack!"

He knew what it would do. He knew now that he had known for a long time what it would do. He had watched it do the same thing over and over again—how many times. And there it was again!

It was a small asteroid, pale pink and delicate, its surface a compound of pools like tinted water and crimson, silky moss. It came out of the heart of the Hive. One moment three green balls had swiveled by and then they parted and the red one shot out. It came at breath-taking speed, spinning madly out, to the very edge of the invisible lines that bounded the Hive. And suddenly it slowed and its spinning slowed and it seemed to float by. It hung quite still, its pools unruffled, its moss calm, and it moved by in slow grandeur, traversing an arc that kept it at the edge of the Hive for a long time. Then as quickly as it had come, it was gone. It turned and re-entered the intricate, alive, complex heart of the Hive.

"You saw it Tom?"

The older man nodded.

"How far from us would you say it passed?"

"Three or four hundredths of a point, maybe."

"Tom," Ames said quietly, steadily, "the next time it comes out—it won't be too long returning—we'll land on it."

"What?" The single word was a harsh, grating sound.

"We'll let it take us into the Hive!" There was no recognition of the older man's fear in Ames voice. "I've watched it come out again and again. If we had known about it from the beginning we could have taken it almost immediately. We need never have stopped the tubes until we were on that—"

"On that crazy asteroid?" Tom cried.

"Exactly. On that crazy asteroid. Don't you see? In that case the Berry gauge would have recorded the trip directly to it and…"

"And what?"

"And somewhere inside the Hive—I don't know where but it must be—somewhere inside there is something that is a distance of point three away! We leave the crazy asteroid to make that little point three jump—and then we've arrived!" His weary eyes were alive again. "And coming back it's the same way. That must be the explanation of the point three jump being duplicated. It *must* be! That crazy asteroid is *the only one* that keeps coming out that way."

TOM had ceased offering resistance. He was too bound up in the mystery, too powerless in the face of Ames' insistence on knowledge, and because he could simply no longer oppose. He nodded gloomily, but he had come out of the half trance-like state in which he had spent most of their hours of standing by. Because of this he became aware of a new peculiar restlessness about Ames.

Ames knew that Tom had noticed it. Waiting to test his hypothesis in action, a new anxiety had arisen. He had calculated his factors with mathematical precision and if he was correct so far he could guess something of the outcome. It was like a man adding a string of sums all ending with the digit five—he might not know the total, but he could foretell that it would end with a five. He had foreseen it before—he had earnestly counted on it—and now he became afraid of it. It might not happen after all. It might happen in an entirely different way. He had not been able to foresee the long hours of waiting here. Was there something else?

"Tom," he said, "I might as well tell you. I've been expecting someone to follow us."

Tom said, "Yeah," in an unquestioning voice. The question followed. "Murchison?"

"Or one of his ambassadors. Still, I don't know. I'm telling you this so you'll be ready if it comes."

Tom nodded. "I'll be ready." He took out his Foster pistol and examined its chambers. Ames, feeling strangely flushed, followed his example. It was an odd sensation, this handling of a deadly weapon with the expectancy—for deep inside him he knew it was more than merely a possibility—of using it. To an unreal world it added another note of unreality. He had to shake that feeling off, he knew. He had enough to think about as it was.

And yet, sitting there, waiting for the exact moment to come when the *Rainbow*'s now throttled but alive tubes would propel her forward on the investigation of a mathematical decision, it did not seem real. It was still a problem on paper. Fighting the notion brought on a heady exhilaration, a recklessness he had seldom known before. He had never considered himself a man of action—not in terms of violence. The world he knew came into contact with the vast, powerful, subterranean worlds of violence and lawlessness only to punish offenders, to maintain order. For a man who wielded law books to be handling a gun was something that unsteadied him. Had he been foolish? Should he not have called in men equipped to handle such problems? Had he brushed by Judge Averill's counsel too quickly, too thoughtlessly? The answer lay within the problem. There had been no problem to hand over to anyone else! He had created the problem himself—he was the only one who knew it existed, and he was proving its existence not by reasoning but by acting! And action alone would see it through. He fingered the heavy weapon. His hands felt moist...

AN HOUR and a half later he touched Tom's arm. "Ready," he said through tight lips. The three green asteroids had appeared. They wheeled into view in a triangular arrangement. Some force kept them together but it was not strong enough to keep them in the same order. Always they emerged grouped, but always altered. This time two were close together and the third far back.

The first two began to separate. The third started catching up, then suddenly slowed and held back. The crimson asteroid shot out of the Hive and into the triangle. The green asteroids veered, swung about, and came together in a tight little group as if to avoid the wild speed and eccentricity of the flaming body that hounded them. The crazy asteroid flashed out alone, steadied.

"Now!"

The ship leaped forward, her bow swung three points forward of the port beam to intercept the orbit of the asteroid. She came in neat, slackened, straightened out. The asteroid was beginning to gather speed again. The *Rainbow* started to fall. That small red world below them hardly offered a landing place. Tom's forehead was covered with sweat. His fists knotted but his touch was delicate. The asteroid began to reenter the inner Hive and the *Rainbow* clung to it, diving at it but losing ground.

The red moss was moving ahead, blurring with speed. If the asteroid once lost the tiny vessel, she would be locked in the Hive, alone amidst hosts of great and small bodies moving at fantastic speeds, with no way to judge their course. Disaster was seconds away and Tom acted.

"Hold on!" he cried.

The *Rainbow* was three hundred feet above the asteroid. Her bow tilted up sharply and her bow tubes roared in sudden violence. The ship kicked back and she dropped and her stern buried itself in the red moss. Tom's quick maneuver had yanked the ship out of space and stuck it stern first into solidity.

So quickly had it been accomplished that both men were still waiting for the shuddering impact to hit them through the bulkheads when the ship was already fast. There had been hardly any sensation of impact at all. The soft viscous earth and moss had cushioned the ship as she fell and sucked her in.

Ames was about to speak, to congratulate Tom—he understood the maneuver had been imperative and magnificently executed, for it had also preserved the ship's ability to blast out, where a bow-dive might have buried her too deeply—but he could not speak. For the asteroid was now in the Hive and accelerating. It swung about insanely, rushing past body after body, turning and twisting, ever on the point of colliding and just veering off.

The half-hour that followed was a nightmare. In the wild images that flashed through Ames mind there was a dim recollection of boyhood terrors on a roller coaster. Ames kept himself from shouting—he might have screamed—only with the knowledge that the asteroid had come out of the Hive every time. It was only when he remembered that it was the collisions of these bodies that produced the vacuum impacts that made what the miners called "bad weather" that he knew fear. For it was possible, always possible, that they would collide. There would be a vast sound, perhaps flame, then nothing. They would never see it, they would never feel the heat or know the impact. The cataclysm would be entered on weather logs...but it is absurd to fear it if this course had been traveled so often, as he thought, before...and yet their ship, small as it was, might upset the delicate balance that had preserved this crazy bit of earth and water and moss...but then why hadn't other ships done so...

GREEN and yellow and gray, balls and slivers, islands of every shape, they bore down on the red traveler to destroy it and lost heart. Immense forms blotted out the sky. Strange shapes danced and lunged and came along and were gone. Then, little by little, they grew less and there was sky again and space again. The asteroid stopped twisting and grew calmer as if from exhaustion.

Not far off—how far away?—lay a quiet asteroid, quite alone. It was mostly brown but spotted with green and blue, and great streaks of black traversed its surface. Black...dull, velvety black, as orium was black...And the green was vegetation, trees and grass, and the blue was water. This still world, perhaps fifty times the size of the red asteroid, lay tranquil within the heart of the Hive—no, it was the heart of the Hive. The mad whirling worlds around it were jealous guards of its peace, sentinels and executioners together, shielding it from possible view. How far had they traveled into the Hive? It was impossible to know. They knew only that it was there.

When the two exhausted, fear-shaken men regarded each other they knew what each thought.

Ames managed to speak. "How far from here is it?"

Tom nodded grimly. "About point three, I reckon."

THERE was no need for further speech. Both knew they could not tell when the red asteroid would swing away again to resume its insane orbit. The method in its madness was plain. Tom touched the controls and the aft tubes and the answering roar shot bits of red moss and earth into space. The *Rainbow* tore herself loose from the embrace of the soft earth and blasted aloft. She soon reached her objective, circled once and settled down to a gentle landing, standing off with her bow pointing up fifteen degrees.

Neither man moved for a few moments. The presence of vegetation, in many places lush and beautiful, generally guaranteed oxygen enough to support human life. Yet the System knew its oddities—and they had not yet identified the vegetation.

They looked out of the bow ports. The *Rainbow* had come to rest on a sandy plain within a shallow valley. The sides of the valley rose leisurely in every direction save one, and that one led to a granitic black-brown series of hills perhaps a mile or so off. A small woods was nearby, and there were winged creatures overhead. Outside, directly ahead of the ship, was a tall, spiny *tono*-grass waving lazily in the wind.

Already there was no sign of the red asteroid; it had gone off to complete its erratic orbit around this haven of quiet. Tom reached for the compartment that housed the sub-atmosphere suits when Ames stayed his hand.

Tom followed the direction of Ames' eyes. There was something moving in the *tono*-grass—moving the spiny laces against the wind. A moment later a shadow appeared among the thick rootstalks and a dark, shaggy head peered out at them. Then slowly, a small black Scotch terrier came walking across the plain towards the ship.

Tom sucked in his breath. "I know that dog," Tom said. "His name's Duke—he belonged to Scotty Purdom."

He got up quickly and led the way to the hatch, opened it and climbed out into the sunlight and the quiet warm wind. Ames followed.

CHAPTER ELEVEN

AT THE first sign of life aboard the ship, the dog fled headlong to the tall grass. Tom and Ames jumped down to the sandy plain and stood there, searching the grass. After a few moments they saw the little terrier inching forward. Its every movement was quick and nervous, and above all, cautious. It peered at the two men from beneath shaggy brows, its ears cocked, its muscles taut. It looked wild, somehow.

"Here, Duke!" Tom called.

At the first syllable, Duke sprang out of sight. If he still moved in the grass, it was with such practiced care that he remained undetected. Tom turned his puzzled face toward Ames. From the moment he had seen the dog, that expression had settled on him like a mask.

"That's Scotty's dog," he said again. "He was always a friendly little feller...not much like..." He let his voice die out because his thoughts were obviously elsewhere. Then he said, "You came here expectin' to find Scotty, didn't you?" His hands fumbled with a field glasses case.

Ames nodded. "Hoping," he said.

"You think he's been hiding here?" He's still somewhere—"

"No," Ames interrupted, sadly; He was still searching for the dog. "If there was a chance that we'd find him here alive—if I ever believed it was possible, and I don't think I did—that dog of his convinced me he's dead." He met Tom's gaze. "Don't you see how that dog acted? It isn't just that he's—well, unfriendly. He's like some animal that never was tamed—and that's because he's been alone for a long time now. If Scotty were still alive somewhere near here, that dog would have run off to him."

"But how would—"

"Look over there," Ames interrupted.

The dog had appeared on the edge of the steepest incline from the valley. He sat flattened out against the horizon, watching them. "That dog's learned to fear men," Ames said, watching Tom as the latter trained his field glasses on Duke.

"You're right," Tom said. He held the glasses in his hand. "Someone shot at him. He's got part of an ear nicked and his left hindquarter's covered with dried blood. But I don't think he's afraid. He looks more to me as if he's waiting to see what we'll do."

"Mmmmm," Ames nodded. "Maybe. Let's follow him."

"You think he'll lead us to Scotty?"

"In spite of himself, yes. I think he'll try to keep between Scotty and us. If he falls back and gets on our flank, that means we're wrong and he's letting us go ahead. But if he runs ahead...we'll see."

They began to execute the plan. The moment they started up the long incline, Duke leaped up and was gone. When they reached the summit, the dog was out of sight. Ames led the way towards the woods. They were halfway there when Tom spotted Duke far to the right. He had been hidden behind a small boulder. Abruptly they changed course. Duke ran across a stretch of wild medicine grass on a tangent toward the hills in the distance and disappeared again. They didn't see him again for perhaps five minutes. He had been behind them and to their left, and he was running, not fast and crouching, ahead of them.

"It's the hills," Ames said. "I'm pretty sure now."

THEY set a straight course for the nearest of the hills, and once they did that they had little trouble keeping Duke in sight. He would lie down and hide and wait somewhere along their path, only to get up and run ahead when they were close to him. But each time he ran a bit slower, and waited longer, so that the distance between them decreased steadily as they came to the hills. Now the dog would stand up and let them see him as he faced them.

Tom said, "He knows it's all up with him. He's makin' up his mind whether or not to attack us, poor little feller."

When they reached the first hill, Duke was near enough for them to hear him growl. They paid little attention to him now. The mineral make-up of the hill was testimony enough. The rich chocolate earth was streaked with black veins that were pure surface orium. Behind the first hill rose others, higher, some sheer outcroppings of soil and rock almost entirely black. There above a jagged overhang stood Duke, some twenty feet over them and fifty feet away. He barked loudly and his eyes looked dark and savage. The two men climbed closer. Duke hid again.

The hills were great disordered masses of rocky boulders through which Nature's hand had sprinkled powdery orium with a lavish hand. The incredible richness of these often-solid boulders was beyond anything Tom had ever heard of. It was scarcely necessary to mine here—all one had to do was take the orium from the surface. Their feet made crunching sounds as they ascended what they soon saw was one of a series of miniature mountains forming a crested semi-circle. Had they been able to perceive this arrangement before, they might have skirted the base of the hills and entered through the open ends of the crescent, but they were already close to the top.

Suddenly they heard Duke barking savagely. The short sharp sound echoed and re-echoed wildly among the boulders, coming from some distance away. Ames ran to the summit as fast as he could.

There, barely visible on the horizon, lay a fairly small spaceship. Below, in the horseshoe-shaped valley formed by the hills, were the shafts and cranes and tunnelers of a mine. Close by the main mine shaft a copter had landed. The barking seemed to be coming out of the large mineshaft. It was followed in a second by a man's hoarse cursing voice, and a second after that by the unmistakable slight, whistling *ping* of a heat pistol, magnified many times by its echo. The dog's barking stopped. A moment afterward its dark, shaggy form came racing out of the mineshaft and a man tumbled out after it.

Ames took all this in, in the time it would have taken him to wink an eye. The vessel, the copter, the man—these three discoveries and their meaning were lost on him. He was still standing there, looking down at the inexplicable scene, when Tom, who had climbed up beside him, shouted down: "Throw them hands up—*fast!*"

The man had his back toward them. He had been holding his right hand stretched out by means of a supporting left hand, and in the evidently crippled right hand he held a Foster pistol. At Tom's voice he wheeled and fired the shot he had been about to send after Duke. He had no surprise on his lean, dark face, and no fear.

Black earth shot up in a cloud at Ames' feet and Ames went down from Tom's shove. The following shot burnt the air where Ames had stood. Tom, flat on his stomach, fired once, twice, three times, his Foster making its tiny clicking release noise. Then he got up on an elbow and swore. "Duck! He's coming up!"

It made no sense to Ames, not until he saw the copter rising in midair. Then he realized that the man had gotten to the waiting copter and was flying up to get at them. In that moment, had Ames gotten up or had he given Tom some sign that he was all right, either man could have fired half a dozen rounds into the momentarily exposed copter. By the time both realized it, the copter had disappeared behind a ridge on their left and almost at their level.

PERILOUS instants ticked by. Ames had taken out his own Foster and opened the safety. He was crawling towards a protecting boulder when the copter shot out horizontally, flying from one ridge to another. Tom sat up and put a hole through its bronzed tail before it disappeared, but from the nose had come a deadly swift succession of tiny gleams of light, the air shimmering all around—the sign of a repeating gun fixed on a bow swivel in the copter. Its beams of heat ate more than halfway through the rock that shielded Tom, forcing him to move.

The copter's game was clear. It could not fire at them openly despite its overwhelming advantage of firepower, but it could keep circling them, flanking their cover, itself covered by one ridge after another. The ridges were like the points of a crown; the copter could shuttle from one to another with a minimum of risk until it caught them between covers. And its machined Foster made all but the heaviest cover untenable.

Again and again the copter darted about the range. Its fire had destroyed most of the upper boulders and Tom and Ames had both been forced to seek cover lower down.

The third time the copter appeared, Ames fired and parted a wing strut. He was amazed to hear himself laughing. It didn't sound like him. He dug in and pulled his long legs in behind him. He had lost sight of Tom.

"Tom!" he shouted. "You all right?"

"Fine! Take care of yourself! Keep separated!"

Sure, sure, that was it. They could creep around to outflank the copter...if they lasted that long. The next time the copter appeared Ames saw that its occupant had thrown back the glassite hatch to increase his visibility. He was aware of what his opponents were doing. He took new steps. Suddenly the copter swooped up, spun on its side and came down at an angle, sweeping the ridge. He was after Ames. His shots had come so close that they burned away the supporting edges of Ames' rock. The rock moved a bit, loosened, and rolled downhill, leaving Ames out in the open. The copter was wheeling back. Something hit its open hatch cover and made the occupant swerve. Ames, standing up, was following the copter with an outstretched, steady arm. He knew his Foster had cut its mark in the copter. But it was Tom's good shooting that saved him then, giving him time, as the copter swerved, to find new shelter. But he was going lower and lower, and as his own shelter grew less, that of the copter multiplied. It came down after him relentlessly and Tom was forced to come down too.

It was a question of time, nothing more. A strange exhilaration had come to Ames, a sort of intense peace. He found himself trying to analyze it and cursed himself for a fool. The copter had dozens of peaks to choose from now. It could move from one to another without being detected half the time, giving it the advantage of surprise when it attacked. And its attacks were more frequent now, and closer. It needed one short burst at close range to end the unequal duel.

The copter slid out from behind a nearby crag and dipped swiftly into the valley, its bow gun flickering. Moments after it was lost from view Ames could still see mad clouds of black dust swirling upward. The copter's persistence could only mean that somewhere below it had caught Tom without protection. Ames pulse was like a hammer as he jumped up to circle around to where he could see the copter, now halfway down the valley and momentarily below him. He forgot his own danger, intent on a glimpse—and then he saw it!

It was less than a hundred feet away, less than thirty feet below his level. Its rotor blades held it in position against the side of a hill that it was eating away. The figure of its driver was low in the seat. Ames raised his gun, and as his arm came up, the dark, quick-moving form of Duke appeared, crawling along the crest of the hill just above the copter. The animal moved with cunning, its form blending into the black hill. It reached a point directly above the driver. A single leap through a few feet of air—it landed within the open hatch of the machine. The dog's snarl mingled with the man's scream as the teeth sank into the back of his neck.

The copter plunged into a neighboring peak, rebounded, hit its rotor blades against rock. The blades splintered off and the copter was lifeless. It crashed over against the hill, dropped twenty feet and kept rolling all the way down into the valley...

CONSCIOUSNESS was returning to the man. Ames laid the man's head on one of the copter's seat cushions and opened his collar. His dark, lean face was turning sallow and bloodless from the draining severed femoral artery that Tom had tourniqueted.

"You're sure?" Ames asked.

"Sure? I've known him since he became Murchison's chauffeur—it's Big Nate Webber, all right."

Ames rose quickly. "Stay with him, Tom. Do what you can and remember this—he mustn't die!" Ames' face was flushed through its weary lines, his eyes looked maddened. "You've got to keep him alive, do you understand?"

He didn't hear what Tom said as he made his way through the tangled wreckage of the copter and began running uphill. A few yards farther up he came upon the mutilated body of the little terrier, where it had fallen, already dead, from the copter during its mad plunge. He kept running as fast as he could, picking his way among the crags, climbing quickly to the summit.

There he made out the *Rainbow* and he plunged downhill toward it. Breathless, his legs like rubber, he ran on. The small ravines and crevices so easily avoided on their upward climb were hidden enemies now and he fell several times. Disheveled, gasping, he reached the plain and kept going without a stop until he came to the ship. He clamored in and quickly gathered up a first aid kit, an electric torch, some sheets of paper and a pen, two canteens of water, and then he was on his way back. Staggering now, he kept his long legs moving, unmindful of the burning dust in his lungs, the stabbing effort to breathe. He climbed the hills again and tumbled, more than ran, down into the valley marked with wrecked machinery. And all the while his brain turned over the unanswered questions, groping for answers. What could he have been thinking of? How had this unforeseen thing been possible? *Unforeseen!* It was a mockery. It had destroyed his plans...*his plans*...but not yet, he told himself, not yet...not yet..."

They worked on Webber for half an hour before his breathing had any strength in it, but Ames knew it was close to the end. The strength and vitality that had kept this man alive through a crushing, smashing fall that had completely destroyed a thing of metal was being sapped by internal injuries over which they had no control. Minutes, perhaps a few hours at most, remained to him.

Webber's eyes were open. There was reason in them. He stared at Tom, watching him as fresh bandages were applied. There was hatred and cruelty in those eyes as Ames raised his head to give him more water. This time less of it dribbled down his chin. His lips moved silently, then his voice came, soft, harsh, venomous.

"You'll...be...paid...off..."

AMES looked down at him. "Save your strength," he said sharply. "You'll need it. It's a long way back to Mirabello." He caught Tom's surprised glance and frowned a warning.

The bloodless lips curled in a slow sneer. "Quit...kidding me...Jack. This...is...the...last...stop... for...me..."

Ames met his eyes and laughed quietly. "It is if I want it to be. I haven't made up my mind yet."

A feeble, foul oath dribbled out of the pale lips.

"You're making it up for me," Ames said, matter-of-factly. He paid no more attention to Webber. He capped the canteen and stood up and walked away a few feet. He sank down on a rock and rested, watching Webber, wondering how successfully he had planted the seed. It wasn't until Tom called him a few minutes later that Ames began to hope again. He returned to the dying man, steeling himself for his obnoxious part, hating himself for the bitter deception. When he looked down at Webber and saw the faint light of hope he had brought to life there, it was almost more than he could bear. But there was no time to lose.

"You're...leveling...with...me...Jack?" Webber asked weakly. Ames nodded and Webber went on. "Really think...I'll...come...out of...this...okay?"

Ames shrugged then. "If you call twenty years in prison okay," he said, "and if I take you back." He hesitated. "Unless you gave me good reason to take you back."

"Rat...on...Murchison?"

"That's right."

The sneer returned. "—you," Webber said.

"All right," said Ames. "I'll put it to you this way. If you had a hand in killing Purdom, I'll get you the best deal—"

Webber tried to laugh. His contemptuous eyes closed.

Ames fought despair. He weighed the gamble; if he was wrong he had lost nothing. Webber was too secure, and part of that security lay in his decision that Ames would not let him die there, that he would be taken back anyway. And had there been hope for him, Ames realized, Webber would be right. He could not convince him otherwise. But suppose the rest of his security was taken away—the security that depended on the knowledge that Murchison was safe? Webber had been Murchison's chauffeur. Was it not possible that the tremendous confidence these men had had in themselves—still evident in Webber's refusal—had that confidence made them commit the error Ames had scarcely hoped to find? To have lost the gamble later would have been a disappointment, but here was a chance to use the possibility that he was right. It was a tiny chance, but it was all he had now.

"Tom," said Ames. "You saw that ship out there? Is that one of Murchison's?"

"Uh-huh. It's his private one."

"Then that's the one he used going to and from the convention at Church's Planet." As Ames spoke, Webber's eyes opened. "That's the one I told Sheriff Kaine about. The Berry gauge in it is what we want." He got up and nodded to Webber. "See what I mean?" he asked softly.

Webber kept staring at him. Presently his lips moved. "What's...the...deal...Jack?" he whispered.

Ames felt his heart throbbing wildly. "Tell us what you know and sign a confession. We'll take you back and do what we can for you." Even then he had been unable to state the cruel lie.

He waited.

After a long pause, Webber said, "You...win..." He began talking then, in a low, hesitant voice. Ames sat near his head, taking the words down, pausing occasionally to give Webber more water, to raise his head. Tom sat silent, listening. The minutes fled by, each taking a little of Webber's strength with it. His voice grew lower and lower, until Ames finally told him to stop. He had heard the one thing he had not known. He wrote swiftly, putting down the last of it ...

"...*Scotty must have seen us coming. We had to follow him down into the mine. He probably didn't know who we were at first, but even after Murchison yelled down to him, he wouldn't come out. Murchison went down. He didn't come up until half an hour later and he told me he had killed Scotty but he couldn't get him out because the gun ate through some shoring and it caved in. Then we went on to Church's. After the convention we came back and took Scotty's and Wylie's ships. We put the bomb Murchison got from Lola into Scotty's ship and waited…"*

"He's goin' fast," Tom whispered.

AMES stopped writing. He put an arm under Webber and raised him up. "Webber, you've got to sign this now," Ames said. He put the pen in Webber's limp fingers. "Sign it," Ames pleaded.

Webber's eyes were glazed. He gripped the pen feebly and let it go again. "Tired—now…" he mumbled. "Later…" But when Ames put the pen in his hand again, he stared at the paper and began to scrawl a huge N. Ames removed his hand and started him again. He wrote his name in a hopeless tangle of letters.

"You've got to do better than that," Ames insisted desperately.

Something in his voice penetrated the thick fog that now separated Webber from the two men. A strange light flared in those dead eyes and fixed itself on Ames. He kept his head from rolling with the remnants of his control. He wet his lips with a thick tongue. "What's…wrong?" he asked. His breath was sluggish now but he forced it to form words. "I'm…dying…" he panted. The realization lit his face with a pallid glow and his lips curled a little to a semblance of a snarl. "You…dirty…double crossing…son …of…a…bi…" His mouth remained open as his head dropped limp against Ames' chest.

Ames laid him down gently and got up. He felt shaken through and through. For many minutes he sat on a rock nearby. He was unaccustomed to violent and ugly death. He sat there until Tom came to him.

"Wasn't pretty," Tom said. "Not even for a human

rattler. I feel a lot worse about that little dog. Guess he saved our lives." After a moment he asked, "Reckon that confession's goin' to help Buck any?"

Ames sighed. "I'm not worried about Wylie. I had more evidence than I need to clear him."

"Then what is it?"

"It's still the confession. It did one thing for me—it told me that it was Murchison himself who committed the murder. But it won't convict him. The signature's unrecognizable and our testimony's objectionable because we're prejudiced."

"What about the Berry gauge in his ship?"

Ames shook his head. "It's a magnificent stroke of luck, and even then it's not enough. Proving where his ship was doesn't prove he was aboard it at the time." He thought a moment. "But it's my one crack at nailing him. I've got him tied with a hundred strings and that's the strongest string of all—but it's still string, and you can't generally hang a man with string. We'll see." He shrugged and said, "Let's have a look in the mine. After what Webber said I don't expect much."

They walked along the valley floor to the main shaft. The heavy odor of smoldering wood was testimony to Webber's confession that he had been destroying shoring to hide what remained of Scotty Purdom, when the dog, faithful to the last, had left two potential marauders for an actual one. Gingerly they lowered themselves. It was several minutes before they came to the smoky passage thirty feet below.

They looked at the decaying remains of Purdom, or what little of him showed. For the lower three-fourths of his body lay buried under a huge slab of orium. The solid block was almost pure. In itself it was worth a king's ransom. There was a tragic irony in the death of this little man, imprisoned by his own incredible wealth, entombed in his famous and secret Silver Spoon Mine.

"This is why Scotty's body wasn't aboard his ship when they set it loose with one of Wylie's bombs in it. They couldn't get him out—"

Suddenly the earth trembled. The dank, smoky cavern shivered and columns of dust loosed themselves in a choking, blinding flood from the mine walls and floor and the hollow reverberations of a thunderous explosion filled the mine. A second roar welled up and the world shook. The timbers on all sides groaned and sagged a little and the dust grew thicker. After the first bewildered moment of panic, when Ames looked up he saw that the shaft above them was still clear and unblocked. Light like an opaque haze still streamed down to supplement the illumination provided by his electric torch. Whatever had happened, it had not been in the mine.

They saw what it was a moment after they reached the surface. Murchison's spaceship was gone. In its stead remained a huge, raw crater over which black and brown clouds of fine earth were still settling. Bits of the blasted ship were scattered around for a mile.

The two explosions had completely demolished it.

PRESENTLY, Ames said, quietly, "That's that, I suppose. I didn't give Murchison credit enough. In the end he thought of everything—even of disposing of Webber and the ship—and its Berry gauge. Those bombs were well timed. If Webber had been aboard somewhere in space he'd be floating jelly. And if he were still here, presumably having killed us as he was sent to do, he'd remain here until he starved to death or until Murchison decided to come and kill him."

"Yeah," Tom nodded. "I guess we're goin' to have to be satisfied with just gettin' Buck out. It's hard to beat a man who destroys part of the evidence, impounds the rest, and then goes ahead and manufactures his own evidence to do tricks for him."

They returned to where Webber's body lay only after two fruitless hours of searching for some possible remnant of the blasted vessel's Berry gauge. With spades they took from the mine they began to dig two graves, one for a man, one for a small animal. They hardly spoke at all. Ames worked automatically, glad of the physical exertion to give his mind some reprieve from its tortuous wanderings and explorations. He had given up, but his mind persisted in returning to the cold body of the case, poking the dead carcass. He had to talk to relieve himself.

"This is one instance where the *corpus delicti* is really the corpse," he told Tom. "You know, there's a general misconception that *corpus delicti* refers to a body. It doesn't. It really means the body of the case, of which the corpse is an integral part. Well, here's a dead body of a case. Or is the joke too academic?"

He went on like that until he realized that he was talking nonsense, and when he fell silent again, he kept thinking. There was really nothing to be done. It was just as Tom had put it—Murchison couldn't be beaten because he played according to his own rules. He either hid evidence by impounding it...*but Ames had gotten around that, hadn't he?* ...or he destroyed it...*but sometimes one might resurrect something with circumstantial evidence of its past existence*...or he manufactured his own evidence to do tricks for him...*but that didn't stop the other side from doing the same...or did it...and if so, why?*

"Why what?" Tom asked.

Ames looked up, startled, and realized he had asked the question in a loud voice. He looked greatly puzzled by what was going on in his own mind, as if he were thinking not merely strange thoughts, but strangely patterned thoughts—thoughts of a nature that had never had a chance to enter his mind and establish some kind of pattern, so that he might recognize them when they returned. No, this was something new. He had never thought of it that way.

"I'm still doing it wrong," he said to Tom, not caring that his meaning was completely beyond Tom. "I listened to everything Averill told me and I thought I'd learned. I lectured him once on going beyond or aside of the law to enforce an essential justice. And what am I still doing? I'm still collecting facts and forgetting people!" He was fairly shouting now. "As far as facts go I've got enough to scare the hell out of him. I've got him even if I can't prove it—but can he be sure of that? Can he possibly be sure when I start throwing facts at him? Will he be able to tell the difference if—"

"Take it easy," Tom gulped, getting hold of Ames' waving arm. "You look like you might blow a valve. Now calm down and let's hear what this thing is that's got you goin' wild."

"I don't know," Ames said, his eyes shining. "I mean I haven't decided on the details yet, but that's the least of it—I'm good at details, you know. I've just got the big idea—*the big idea*—the one that's going to do it." He threw down his shovel. "And the first part of it is this: we're not burying either Webber or Duke."

"No? What are we doin' with them?"

"We're taking them back to Mirabello with us. Don't

look at me like that. We'll wrap them in tarpaulin and keep the bodies in the outer chamber where it'll be cold enough to keep them from decomposing. I know it's a messy job but we've got to do it. It's the only—"

"Calm down now, please," Tom begged. "You got me convinced. I'm not sayin' a word, am I? Only get a good grip on yourself."

Ames nodded and sat down. His clothes were wringing with sweat. He couldn't keep his hands still even then. "Whew!" he kept saying...

SOME hours later, when the *Rainbow* had successfully negotiated the return hop to the crazy asteroid when it came around again, Ames and Tom had a chance to check on one of the things Webber had told them. It was almost the only thing Ames hadn't known—that there was a sort of back entrance to the Silver Spoon asteroid. For there was another place on the out-entrance to the Silver Spoon asteroid that emerged long enough to enable a ship to get to it.

They saw the invisible borders of the hive where Webber had come, sneaked in ahead of them, but they remained with the crazy asteroid until it had completed the circuit back to where the *Rainbow* had first landed on it, as Ames put it, "to keep the Berry gauge for the return trip as close as possible to a 76 reading—" and winking, "—got to keep the facts straight."

"Calm down," Tom said. "For the luvva Pete, calm down!"

CHAPTER TWELVE

IT WAS late in the afternoon of August 4th when the *Rainbow* settled her battered hulk into the pits of Standish port. The day was hazy and too warm for Spring, the sun overcast, and there were few people about. Perhaps because of this as well as her own monumental unimportance, the *Rainbow*'s arrival went almost unnoticed. But two hours later, when her owner's representative came to check on her condition, he found her the center of attraction for a growing crowd of mechanics, miners, field officials and various hangers-on.

On the edge of the field two official cars flanked a truck guarded by deputies. There were more deputies around the *Rainbow*, and inside her, among them the unusual figure of Sheriff Kaine. The cars and the truck had come up unheralded and deputies had carried an open coffin and a basket to the ship. When they emerged, the bare wooden coffin was obviously weighted, and it was sealed. The same was true of the basket. Both were quickly taken to the waiting truck.

There was more than enough fuel there to feed the fires of a dozen wild stories. Tom alone was present, and word came from the port officials—quickly seeping through the throng—that he had left with Terwilliger Ames. No one had seen Ames. There was a coffin. There was also a mysterious basket. It was more than enough, but even more was added when Sheriff Kaine refused to let the *Rainbow*'s representative take charge of her. The unhappy, and quickly branded *ill-fated* vessel was impounded, sealed, and blasted off from Standish on an officially supervised journey, undoubtedly to government sheds at Mayville.

It was all over by the time the *Twin-Sun's* reporters and a photographer arrived. Sheriff Kaine was leaving in one of the cars. He had nothing to say; he would not be quoted. The reporters nosed around and heard a hundred stories— except that to their trained ears it did not sound like a hundred stories, but a hundred variations on one story— that Ames had been killed somehow. His body had been carted off together with an important basket of evidence. They discounted the story that Ames' head was in the basket. The rest of it—carefully weighed and pruned and edited—they scribbled in their pads conscientiously.

With the *Rainbow* gone, the news-hawks did the best they could. They went to the Standish port registry files and dug up pictures of the *Rainbow* from her halcyon days. They interviewed the port officials, who knew nothing but suspected the worst, and because of their suspicions and earnest desire to avoid undue publicity of such a sort, they talked altogether too much. The photographer also took a dozen shots of Tom as he stood talking with Kaine just before the sheriff left, and when Tom left, they followed him, begging for an interview, offering bribes and inducements for his story of the supposed tragedy.

Tom listened and sighed and reported only that his tongue was in the sheriff's custody. For reasons which he alone knew, he went to Ames' house in Mirabello City, still followed by the reporters, but before he could enter the house he was met by two men who had come from the city as soon as they had heard the *Rainbow* was back. It turned out they knew nothing else of its return. They were regional representatives of System Ethergraph, Ltd.

They carried copies of a graph sent to the Central

Office many days before by Ames, notifying S. E. that he was filing suit against them under the Communications Statutory Laws, Section 885, for a branch manager's violation. They had been in Mirabello City for three days waiting for the *Rainbow* to return. System Ethergraph was deeply concerned that the esteemed Mr. Ames had cause to complain. When Tom reluctantly told them it was impossible for them to see Mr. Ames, the reporters took it upon themselves to explain why. Tom left the enjoyable scene with misunderstood sadness and went into the house.

There he found the remains of an opulent and fantastic omelet, a thing of which Ames had spoken all the way back. He tiptoed upstairs and had a look at Ames as he slept. Of his desire for a long, undisturbed session in bed too, Ames had spoken with some passion. It was as if he had come out of a prison—as indeed, for so many days he had been the prisoner of his thoughts and unceasing work—to return to normality with a vengeance. A third desire, fishing, had also evoked longing from him. The fourth, though Tom was certain it would have been first had Ames been the man to talk of it, had not been mentioned. He had not uttered Sue's name at all.

Tom waited for the deputies to come, left one to guard the house and left with the other to visit Sheriff Kaine. When he returned some two hours later, he carried two interesting objects. One was a bulky jar covered with heavy foil. The second was a special edition of the *Twin-Sun* on which the ink had scarcely dried. He put them both on Ames' dressing table, bade the guarding deputies goodnight and went to sleep...

THE dawn was announced by a series of shouts from

Ames' room. He had jumped out of the *Rainbow* a moment after it landed, made his way inconspicuously home, called Sheriff Kaine and had half an hour's talk with him. The sheriff had left for the blastport and Ames had gone to sleep immediately. The first he knew of his death was when he read about it the next morning.

Pajama-clad but barefoot, he was rushing down the stairs when he was met by the deputies and Tom. He waved the paper at them incoherently and tried to speak, and finally all he managed to get out were the words:

"Mystery Surrounds Death of Ames!"—which was a strict quotation of the headline. Even before he had spoken, Tom and the deputies were weak with laughter. They hung on the stair railing, bracing each other. Ames stared at them until he began to smile helplessly.

Some minutes later, in the kitchen, he heard the story while he had coffee and read the morning edition of the *Twin-Sun*, which one of the deputies had brought in.

There were two headlines. The first stated: SHERIFF KAINE REFUSES TO MAKE PUBLIC AUTOPSY VERDICT. The second was in red ink underneath: BUREAU OF CLAIMS BARES SECRET PURDOM-WYLIE PARTNERSHIP. The stories that went with both headlines took up most of the paper and Ames devoured them. "My God, listen to this," he read. " '…during the night, a story circulated earlier yesterday and generally discredited gained some credence in view of Sheriff Kaine's unprecedented action in suppressing the coroner's verdict. It was believed possible that the mysterious basket viewed by dozens of witnesses did indeed contain Ames' head, but so badly battered that identification was not immediately possible.' " Ames touched his crown gingerly. " 'Should this prove to be true,' " he read on, " 'the sheriff's action becomes more understandable. It may be that the sheriff will need dental and medical data before the identification is certain. At any rate, Sheriff Kaine's only public statement as to the verdict so far has been: *Gentlemen, the autopsy proves that the corpse is dead...*' "

Ames broke off laughing and went on to the other story. Beside a photo of the *Rainbow*, retouched to make it look grimy with age, was a photo of Colonial Attorney Whitley, under which was his statement: "Naturally I am not free to comment upon matters pertaining to the Wylie trial which begins today, but I can say that the astonishing revelation of the Bureau of Claims is bound to figure prominently in the prosecution's case."

Ames smiled wryly and commented: "To say nothing of the case for the defense once a certain material witness testifies." He sighed and turned a page. "Be a good fellow and make me an omelet, Tom? I want to read some of these touching tributes to me by fellow citizens."

"Ordinary omelet or special?"

"Super. And don't spare the Uranian onions or garlic. I don't want anybody to have any doubts about my being alive." He added, "Does Judge Averill know the truth?"

"Uh-huh. Kaine told him." He went on, with careless emphasis: "Anybody else who might like you still thinks you're dead but not buried."

Ames glanced at him. Presently he put the paper down with a thoughtful smile. "What a wonderful morning this must be for Murchison."

Tom nodded, cracking eggs. "I'm thinkin' you ought to wear a lily in your lapel. I just can't wait for that blessed moment when you march into that courtroom." He sighed. "Soon as you're through eatin' we got a date upstairs with that jar. Remember?"

"Mmmmmm," was Ames' comment. He was lost in thought.

IT WAS almost ten o'clock when the blessed moment for which Tom waited arrived, except that it was more than an affair of a moment. It began almost immediately after Ames left his house. As he rode through the streets of the town in an official car he was seen, and the news spread almost as fast as the car traveled. When the car stopped briefly in the town square before a florist's, Ames was seen going into the shop and coming out. The excitement caught up with him and beat him to the courthouse. By the time he alighted there, a police escort was necessary to get him into the building.

But even Ames had under-estimated what was happening. The halls were crowded beyond Mirabello City's power to crowd them. There were more photographers and reporters than a dozen newspapers could have provided. Flash bulbs popped on every hand and people tried to break through the cordon around him. Blinded and bewildered, he was pushed through a mobbed courtroom into the inner well before the bench. There he was besieged, and presently he began to understand, from what the numerous howling newspapermen were saying, precisely what had happened.

Newspapers from the Group around and from far beyond it had begun to pour their men into Mirabello since the afternoon of the day before. They had come from everywhere by special ship, by chartered clippers, to get in on the case, and more were arriving hourly. The *Twin-Sun's* syndicated scoop of Ames' death had been graphed throughout the System, and the *Twin-Sun* had been even more lurid in its graphed accounts of developments than it had been at home. Stories carried implied tie-ups of his mysterious death and the trial, and of both of these with the news of the Bureau of Claims revelation.

But even this had not quite explained the mass immigration, and certainly not to the equally bewildered newsmen of the *Twin-Sun*. There was more to it. Ames, a brilliant and famous New York lawyer, had disappeared some four months before. The first word of his whereabouts had come when he had ethergraphed for credentials to friends, and then it was known he was in Mirabello. In Mirabello! And what was he doing there? Why had he gone? What lay behind it? And then System Ethergraph's news release that a certain T. Ames had filed, or intended to file, suit for criminal action. And then, filtering through, accounts of his being involved in a murder trial—and finally, his mysterious death on the eve before he was due in court as a material witness, a status he had achieved through an unbelievable series of accusations. What did it mean? What did it add up to?

It added up to what Ames saw, heard and felt all around him—a jammed courtroom, newspapermen, specially leased graph wires in the courthouse, vast noise and excitement, and a police problem. He retreated, muttering, to a chair near the bench and mopped his brow and caught his breath. He straightened out his neat blue suit and adjusted the wild cowlicks of his hair. He sprinkled a dab of water on the lily he had gotten at the florist's, which he wore in his lapel. Finally, when some order had been restored by courtroom attendants, he turned in his seat and glanced around.

CLOSEST to him was the table reserved for the prosecution. Colonial Attorney Whitley and the seven or eight men of his staff were in huddled consultation around it, and as Ames glanced at them, Whitley got up and came toward him. Farther over, at the table for the defense, sat Farley and Buck Wylie, with Lola Morales between them. Several people, among whom Ames recognized witnesses from the indictment proceedings, sat in the first row of seats, near the jury box. As Whitley neared Ames the jury started filing in from its room.

At the same moment, Ames spotted Tom in the third row. He was sitting beside Sue Wylie. Ames saw that the girl had been looking at him from the start; his eyes met hers and locked. Whitley was beside him now, and Ames murmured, "Excuse me," got up, walked to the railing and gave the lily to a court attendant with whispered instructions. The attendant smiled and delivered the lily to Sue Wylie. The delivery, her hesitant smile, and Tom's broad grin were immediately recorded by a dozen popping flashbulbs. Immediately attendants descended on the owners of the forbidden and hitherto secreted cameras, causing a new uproar.

Whitley was saying, "...our congratulations on your being here."

Ames grinned at him. "I couldn't afford not to be here," he told Whitley. "I'm out on five dollars' bail, and the way business has been, I need it."

"Yes, of course," Whitley coughed. "Just the same, I felt—"

He didn't get a chance to finish because Judge Averill's chamber door opened and the judge came out in his robes. The clerk intoned his ancient cry and the quieting courtroom stood until the judge was seated.

The formalities took a few minutes. Averill noted the presence of the C. A. and Farley, attorney of record for the defendant, consulted with both, as well as with members of Whitley's staff and late additions to Farley's. Once glances were directed at Ames. The judge frowned, made a notation and said something that ended the consultation. As the men returned to their tables a hush fell over the courtroom. For the first time the judge looked toward Ames and inclined his head.

The trial began.

Whitley addressed the jury in a quiet, studious manner. He outlined the nature of the case, the prosecution's intentions and touched on witnessed and circumstantial evidence, motivation and penalties. When he sat down, Ames followed his confident gaze to where Murchison was sitting in the second row, directly behind Ames.

By comparison, Farley was ill at ease. He expressed confidence in the jury's ability to decide on evidence and to take the law as directed by the judge. There was a cloying quality in his unsubtle wooing.

One of Whitley's staff, a heavy-set young man named Tisdale took over. He summoned, in order, Harvey Franshaw and Timothy Saunders and led them patiently. It was established that Scotty Purdom had, during the evening of July 9th, phoned Buck Wylie from the Rocketeers Cafe and made an appointment with him for the following morning. On the morning of the 10th, Purdom and Wylie were seen together at the Standish blast port, engaged in conversation. Each then left in his own ship and both headed east together. Both men were seen together later that day. They had returned to Standish port where Purdom fuelled his vessel and again they left together in the two ships, heading northwest.

Franshaw went unchallenged. Saunders was asked by Farley: "Can you, sitting here, tell me which direction is northwest?" Saunders consulted a watch, looked at a window and pointed accurately to northwest.

Tisdale then called a traffic manager from the Standish port. The manager, from ledgers, testified that he had records of two arrivals and departures on July 10th for vessels named Spoon *Special* and *Hellcat*, and that these arrivals and departures had taken place a minute or two apart. The testimony was interrupted by Farley, who objected to a waste of time and conceded that the two ships had come in and left together.

Tisdale smiled, ignored him, and went on with the prosecution's evidently painstaking case. Two Standish attendants testified to fueling the *Spoon Special* on the 10th. Then Tisdale called Larry Mason.

Mason, a middle-aged man, was identified as an employee at the Wylie *arrando* for five months previous, and still employed there. He testified that on the morning of the 10th, he had fueled the *Hellcat* while Purdom and Buck waited. Again Farley objected to a waste of time and offered to concede.

WHITLEY got up. "Your Honor, unless defendant's attorney is also willing to concede defendant's guilt and so plead, I must ask that he be restrained from further interruptions."

Judge Averill said: "The court advises Mr. Farley to examine more carefully what he concedes. The defendant's life in his hands. It may be that the prosecution is establishing a point which defense may not be willing to concede after all."

As if to prove the value of Judge Averill's advice, Tisdale then took a new line. He asked Mason: "Was there enough fuel at Wylie's own port to have fuelled the

Spoon Special too?"

"Yes, sir. Enough to have fuelled twenty ships like her."

"But you did not fuel the *Spoon Special*?"

"No, sir."

"In other words, you fuelled only the *Hellcat*, but the *Spoon Special* was then sent on to Standish port to fuel there?"

"Yes, sir."

Farley was on his feet. "Objection. The witness did not see the *Spoon Special* being fuelled at Standish."

Judge Averill directed: "Strike the question and answer from the record." To Farley he said: "Mr. Farley, you did not previously contest testimony to the effect that the *Spoon Special* was fuelled at the Standish port. Unless you desire, at some point, to offer contradictory evidence, the Court does not understand your correct, though useless, objection."

Farley flushed. "The law is the law," he stated with pettish arrogance. "He had no right to ask that question."

Averill frowned at him, then looked away. "Proceed, Mr. Tisdale."

Tisdale asked: "Do you know why... Strike that out, please. Did you hear anything that might have explained why the *Spoon Special* was not fuelled at the Wylie port?"

Farley was up again. "Object to 'might have explained'."

"Sustained. Witness is not here to venture guesses."

Tisdale asked: "Did you, Mr. Mason, at any time during the fueling, hear anything said by either Wylie or Purdom?"

"Yes, sir. I heard a few things."

"Anything about the fuelling?"

"Yes, sir. Scotty told Mr. Wylie that if he could fuel the

Special right then and there, he'd save time and wouldn't have to go to Standish. Also, I heard him say, 'It's the same money, ain't it?' "

"What did Wylie say to that?"

"He said it would look better if Scotty went to Standish for his fuel. He said there were too many people wondering about them already, and he mentioned that the whole idea annoyed him from the start."

Ames glanced around at the courtroom, partly because he was a little bored with the prosecution's slow development of a theme to prove Buck's partnership with Scotty, partly from interest in what he saw on the faces he regarded. Buck Wylie looked grim but patient, his hand resting on those of the girl beside him. Tom and Sue were attentive, and Murchison, who saw Ames turn toward him, had a benign expression that he did not change for Ames. The lawyers for both sides were engaged in furious scribbling and note passing. He swallowed a yawn.

"To your knowledge, Mr. Mason," Tisdale had asked, "was there ever an occasion on which Wylie did fuel a vessel for Scotty?"

"Yes, sir. About six weeks before that time, Mr. Wylie fuelled the *Hellcat* and let Scotty Purdom take her. I wasn't supposed to know—"

Tisdale stopped him, anticipating Farley as he rose to object, and the latter part of the answer was deleted. Buck Wylie's face showed open rage as he bent to listen to Farley. A murmur had run through the courtroom. Farley got up before Tisdale could resume.

"If the court please, defense agrees and admits the point Mr. Tisdale is so laboriously making. Mr. Wylie admits he was engaged in a partnership with Purdom for several months before Purdom's disappearance."

"Order!" Judge Averill rapped sharply. To Tisdale he said dryly: "Counsel for defense seems impatient, Mr. Tisdale. If the State agrees, Mr. Farley's statement will be entered in the testimony."

WHITLEY expansively signified agreement and Tisdale offered in evidence a certified duplicate of the file claim that day made public by the Bureau of Claims. It was accepted and entered. Tisdale resumed.

"Mr. Mason, what did you do after you fuelled the *Hellcat*?"

"Mr. Wylie and Scotty left, then I fuelled the *Gaucho* like Mr. Wylie told me. Then, it being a Saturday, I went to town."

"Did you see Wylie—"

"That's a lie!" Buck cried. For a moment no one knew what he meant, because he had reacted so slowly to Mason's previous answer. He was standing now, shouting, "I never told him to fuel the *Gaucho!*" He was livid with fury, and only Lola Morales' entreaties finally quieted him down; he paid no attention to Averill's orders. He sat there looking at Mason, lips tightened to a line, dangerous and ugly.

"Mr. Mason, do you remember the day of July 24th?"

"Yes, sir, I do. I have special reasons, of course, what with Scotty's ship being found that day. That was a Saturday and I'd gone to town the night before with the boys, but that morning, about eleven, I came back to the *arrando*, I had a special date in town for the night and I wanted to be dressed up special. About noon, before I left, I saw the *Gaucho* come into our port. Mr. Wylie'd left in her the Sunday before. With him coming back after a long trip I knew that if he or the foreman spotted me, they'd put me to work on her, so I beat it good and fast. I went back to town and that night I heard about Scotty's ship being found adrift over at Grey Mountain."

"And when was the next time you saw the *Hellcat*?"

"The next morning, Sunday, about eleven. She was back at our port. I'd gone back to the *arrando* early because I heard the Sheriff was coming up there with Mr. Whitley and I wanted to be there too."

Tisdale thanked Mason and turned him over to Farley. Farley got up quickly and fixed Mason with a belligerent look.

"On July 10th, the day you fuelled the *Hellcat*, you left shortly thereafter and did not return to the *arrando* until early Monday morning?"

"Yes, sir, that was the custom. We all got back together."

"Then, as far as you know, it is entirely possible that Mr. Wylie returned to his *arrando* shortly after you left and was there all the time until you yourself returned. Is that right?"

"It was possible."

"That's all," said Farley, looking satisfied.

His satisfaction was not mirrored in Buck Wylie's dark, angry face, nor did it last long. Tisdale then introduced three witnesses who were employed by Buck and who substantiated various parts of Mason's evidence. They did not substantiate his statement that Buck had ordered him to fuel the *Gaucho* the day Purdom left, not having been there. None was cross-questioned by Farley. The prosecution then called a Dr. Ballister, expert on explosives, and Whitley himself took over.

As Exhibit A, Whitley submitted to the Doctor's examination the fairly small but extremely heavy and powerful demolition bomb found in the *Spoon Special*. Printing, serial numbers and manufacturer's trademark identified it as one of a large shipment Buck had bought some time before. The expert offered his opinion that it was likely, had the bomb gone off, that it would have been difficult to trace its ownership.

On this point, Farley, in his questioning, got Dr. Ballister to admit that it was *possible* that the ownership of the bomb could have been traced even from fragments the size of a pinhead. The expert left the stand a good deal unhappier than he had taken it.

Whitley then called Harry Reichard. Reichard had seen the *Hellcat* towing the *Spoon Special* off Grey Mountain on the afternoon of the 24th. Farley got Reichard to admit he had not seen who was at the helm of the *Hellcat*.

WHEN old Bob Halloway took the stand, there was an outbreak of scattered applause and a warning from the judge. Whitley had trouble confining his witness to legal evidence, but his story was the same one he had told at the indictment proceedings. He had seen the *Spoon Special* on the evening of the 24th, moving in a slow circle over Grey Mountain. She did not respond to AV signals. He grappled and boarded her, put out a live fuse in a bomb. He identified the bomb. There had been no one aboard the ship. He had called Standish and taken both ships in to port.

Throughout his testimony he kept trying unsuccessfully to tell the crowded courtroom of his personal danger and the injury to his hands. When Farley waived examination and the old man left the stand, new applause broke out. The old man reacted and in a fit of enthusiasm shook a fist at Buck Wylie and shouted: "Damn your hide, if I was a younger man I'd a paid you off fer my hands myself! In my day—"

The rest of it was lost in the uproar. Farley had instantly jumped up and heatedly demanded a mistrial. He was still the last one speaking when order was finally restored.

Judge Averill fixed a stern, inquisitive gaze at him. Curtly, he said: "You know very well, Mr. Farley, that no grounds for a ruling of mistrial exist. Motion denied. The jury will disregard Mr. Halloway's additional remarks. Proceed, Mr. Whitley."

But the even tenor of the trial had been broken. Until that moment it had developed along slow, routine lines, with the prosecution methodically fashioning a noose around Buck Wylie's neck. It had borne out none of the drama it promised; several reporters had sauntered out and others stopped taking notes. Halloway's outburst had charged the room momentarily, and now something occurred to increase the tenseness.

Whitley called John Murchison to the stand and announced him as the last State's witness. Until then Ames, constantly under observation, had shown small interest in the trial. Even Halloway's outbreak had not ruffled his calm. But now he leaned forward in his chair, elbows on the table and his earnest face cupped in his hands, watching Murchison. The courtroom seemed to lean forward with him.

And then Murchison's evidence took a brief three or four minutes. He avowed his partnership with Purdom, sketched in the man's known background. He then reported on Purdom's unfailingly regular habits. That was the point Farley attacked with helpless savagery.

"Will you not admit, Mr. Murchison, that there is a

distinct possibility that Scotty Purdom merely wandered off somewhere alone?"

"In what? You mean he sent his ship back magically—"

The answer was stricken out. Answering again, Murchison said, "In my opinion, there is no such possibility. In the years I knew him, he never once deviated from habit. Why should a man of such great wealth merely wander off? Unless you can produce testimony that he was insane, and I defy you—"

"That will be all, Mr. Murchison," Judge Averill broke in. "Mr. Farley, the Court expects you to confine the State's witnesses to testimony, not to conjectures and challenges, which, if allowed to continue, might very definitely damage the defense of this case. It should not be necessary for the Court to undertake your functions."

Farley, deeply flushed, seemed unable to go on. After a moment he dismissed Murchison. As he walked back to his table and Ames leaned back in his chair with a grin on his face, a loud buzz swept the courtroom. Every eye was fixed on Farley as he sat down. Buck Wylie's head was down. He did not seem to be listening to the lawyer on his right who was whispering to him.

Whitley's voice was satisfied. "The State rests, your Honor."

JUDGE AVERILL nodded and consulted his watch. The prosecution had presented its tight case in a little over two hours, an astonishing feat. It was a quarter past twelve. After a momentary hesitation, the judge asked if there were any witnesses for the defense.

Farley spoke to the lawyer who had been talking to Buck and that young man, named Brent, rose and gave a name to the clerk. The name, Godfrey Loomis, was called and a tall, well-dressed man came to the stand. He was sworn in and Brent quickly established him as an official of the Bureau of Claims.

"Precisely what do you do for the Bureau, Mr. Loomis?"

"I am an investigator for the Commerce Division. My work consists of checking all filed claims to see that the claimed locations exist, that they have been properly marked, and do not infringe on other claims that may be in the vicinity."

"In other words, you are a sort of detective?"

"Well, yes, you might say so."

"And you have had long experience and are skilled in your work?"

"I think I can safely say so."

"Mr. Loomis, will you describe to the jury the nature and findings of your work from July 29th to August 3rd?"

"I came here to Mirabello City on July 29th at Mr. Wylie's request to undertake an examination of certain areas. In all, I visited six places named and located by Mr. Wylie, covering millions of miles. I found at each of these places the official markers of the Bureau for a preliminary claim. Each of them was signed with Mr. Wylie's name and with dates ranging from July 14th to July 23rd. There were also unmistakable evidences of recent habitation at each of these places."

"What would you call evidence of such habitation?"

"The markers were all new and unaffected by weather. Also there were fireplaces with the ashes still intact in several instances."

"Would you, Mr. Loomis, say from these evidences that Mr. Wylie had been at these places—"

"Objection!" Tisdale called. "Witness is being asked a

question he cannot possibly answer unless he saw Mr. Wylie there with his own eyes."

"Sustained."

Brent nodded and asked: "Did any of the places you visited take you within fifteen million miles of the Lydonna Group?"

"No, they did not."

Brent then offered in evidence a sworn deposition, concurred in by two accompanying witnesses, enumerating the places visited and their relative distances from the Lydonna Group and Mirabello. After that Tisdale took the witness.

"You are a detective, Mr. Loomis?"

"Well, sort of."

"What is your official classification?"

"Claim adjuster."

"Have you ever performed duties which you could call detective work and has the Bureau ever used your services in such a capacity?"

"Well, that depends on what you call detective work."

"Have you ever been called on to testify in any criminal action by the Bureau which involved your own special findings?"

"Only insofar as they pertained to claim infringement."

"Were professional detectives also called on in these actions?"

"Yes."

"Then it would appear that the Bureau does not consider you a competent substitute for such professional detective work?"

"I...ah...well, you might say so."

"Could you swear that the fireplaces and ashes were not a week or two or possibly even three weeks older than you guessed they were?"

"Well, I don't know if I'd swear to it. After all, I'm not a—"

"A professional detective, you mean? We've already established that, Mr. Loomis," said Tisdale with a warm smile. "Now, would you be willing to swear that it was Mr. Wylie who put up those markers *himself?*"

"I don't see how I could."

"Neither do I," Tisdale smiled again. "One more question. As far as you know, *couldn't* someone else have put those markers?"

"Well, yes...certainly it's possible."

STILL smiling, Tisdale excused the distressed witness and sat down. There was a pause before Farley got up. He seemed only partially recovered from his earlier discomfiture. He turned toward Lola Morales and motioned her to the stand. She was waiting. She squeezed Buck's hand and walked up confidently. Her sultry beauty had its effect on the spectators and she acknowledged their murmurs from under shaded lashes.

Farley proceeded cautiously with her. His chief difficulty seemed to be concerned with her residence at the Wylie *arrando*. He finally established that she was a "friend" of Buck's who had been staying at the *arrando* on an extended visit. Farley went on.

"Miss Morales, tell us what you remember of the events of July 10th. You recall the day, I assume?"

"Perfectly. He left the *arrando* early that morning and returned before noon with Mr. Purdom. Then both of them left. About two o'clock I saw the *Hellcat* come in. Mr. Wylie came to the house and the *Hellcat* took off again. Mr. Wylie told me that Mr. Purdom was using his ship."

"How long did Mr. Wylie stay home?"

"Until Sunday, July 18th, eight days later, when he left in the *Gaucho* on his usual prospecting trip. He always went the third week of every month."

"When did you see him again?"

"Just before noon on the 24th. He returned in the *Gaucho*."

"Now, Miss Morales, I want you to be very careful in answering my next question: Did he go out again that day, the 24th?"

"He definitely did not."

"You were in a position to have known had he gone out?"

"Most certainly. We were together all that afternoon and evening until quite late that night." Gratuitously she added, "We spent the afternoon listening to a concert."

Her last remark elicited a ripple of laughter that brought her up defiantly in her chair. Farley blushed, cleared his throat and went on, speaking loudly and carefully. "In other words, Miss Morales, you know that Mr. Wylie was home by noon of the 24th and stayed there?"

"Most certainly."

Farley indicated he was through and Tisdale advanced to the girl with a serene and polite expression.

"Miss Morales, how long have you been staying at the *arrando*?"

"I'm not sure."

Tisdale smiled. "You seemed quite sure about dates a minute ago, Miss Morales. A month? Six months? A year? How long?"

"A little over six months."

"Rather a long visit, isn't it?"

Over a few titters from spectators, the girl raised her

voice harshly. "What if it is? What's that to you?"

"Nothing, I'm sure," Tisdale said quickly. "Do you have any other address, Miss Morales?"

"Not at present."

"Are you related to Mr. Wylie in any way?"

"We're good friends," the girl said, growing angry again.

"May I ask whether you have ever been engaged in any occupation?"

"I have never had a job, if that's what you mean. Is all this necess—?"

"May I inquire as to the source of your income?"

Through clenched teeth the girl answered in a level voice: "I inherited a million dollars from a dead lawyer. Cold cash."

Tisdale's smile flashed again, briefly. "Miss Morales, you say you're a good friend of Wylie's. With no offense meant, and taking into consideration that you are testifying under oath, may I ask whether you might consider—ah— fibbing, to protect him?"

"Objection!" Farley cried. "Witness is under oath."

"Strike out the question," the Judge ordered. "Mr. Tisdale, the Court will not allow you to address insinuations to the jury under guise of examining a witness. The jury will disregard the question."

Tisdale looked humbled. He hesitated a moment, then looked up at the girl and shot at her: "Isn't it true that Buck Wylie has been keeping you? Isn't it true that he pays all your bills, buys your clothes, gives you money? Aren't you Buck Wylie's mistress?"

LOLA MORALES jumped off the chair and swung a resounding smash into Tisdale's face. She was restrained from following it up only by the quick action of a court attendant. Buck was standing, trembling with poorly controlled rage, while two lawyers held him. Judge Averill rapped his gavel and threatened to clear the courtroom if there was another outburst from the spectators.

Tisdale, safely across the inner well, demanded: "What about an answer to that question, Miss Morales? Isn't it true?"

Lola Morales stood up and said in a loud voice: "No, it isn't, you damned, dirty, lying lawyer! It isn't true!"

It took another five minutes to quiet the courtroom again. Tisdale had signified he was through with the witness and the prosecution's table looked expectantly from Farley to Judge Averill. Quiet was finally restored only because Farley made an announcement that astonished the courtroom.

"The defense has no more witnesses to call, Your Honor."

The judge shook his head. "It's just as well. I was about to declare a recess. This afternoon, when Court reconvenes, the State will summarize…you're out of order, Mr. Ames! Sit down, please!"

Ames remained standing. He had gotten up a moment after Farley closed the case for the defense. "Your Honor, if you adjourn this session now and begin the next one with the State's summary of the case, I won't have had my chance to speak here. Therefore, I must risk—"

"Your Honor, I object!" Whitley thundered. "Mr. Ames has no—"

"He has no right to volunteer evidence!" Farley cried.

"—I must risk," Ames continued, "the Court's displeasure by now speaking out of order. I petition your Honor that I be heard."

All through this triple exchange and shouting, the

courtroom had been hushed. The silence now offered a tense, very dramatic contrast to the previous behavior of the audience. Not a man or a woman there but was on the edge of a seat, waiting to hear Judge Averill.

"Mr. Ames, the Court is aware that you are here as a material witness, both on the application of the State as well as the defense. However, at the beginning of this trial, the Colonial Attorney and counsel for defense notified the Court that in view of later findings, you would not be called for testimony by either side. The Court acknowledges that it is highly unusual for defense counsel, especially, to spurn examination of any testimony that might help his client, or, if he fears damage to his client as a result of such testimony, for the Colonial Attorney to refuse to take advantage of the possibility. However, the Court is bound in this instance and finds it impossible to grant your petition."

"If the Court please," said Ames quietly, "may I respectfully submit contrary finding on appeal to the Colonial Supreme Court, in the case of Ajax Vessels vs. Grant, Volume 12. Also the case of Farwell, Vosseler vs. Mercurian Commonwealth, Volumes 21, 26 and 27. Also the case of Grimes, Grimes and Thackeray vs. Jones, Tyuio Superior Court, Volume 6. Also the special appendix, part 3, of *MacDougal's Interplanetary Torts and Laws*, relative to appeals from a material witness. Also—"

"One moment, Mr. Ames," Judge Averill interrupted, looking up from the rapid notes he had been taking. "Was that part 3 of the special appendix you mentioned?"

"Yes, Your Honor."

His Honor wrote again, put down his pen and looked down at Ames with a pleasant smile. "The Court will take your petition under advisement and render a decision as soon as Court reconvenes. Decision therefore is reserved. This Court stands adjourned until two o'clock."

It was not a moment too soon, for during Ames' listing of references the courtroom had gotten to its feet, biding its time for an outburst. It came before the Judge had taken his smile with him to his chambers. Reporters swarmed around Ames, hurling questions at him, asking his opinion, pushing him back against the wall.

He was saved only by Sheriff Kaine's quick action and his announcement of a small luncheon for the visiting newspaper people, who numbered a mere fifty or so. Sue Wylie and Tom were among those present, but they were at the other end of the table. And as Amos parried questions and kept looking toward them, his expression was, in the words of one astute reporter, "—he looks at that dame as if he wanted to eat her instead of that omelet he ordered."

CHAPTER THIRTEEN

PRECISELY at two o'clock, in an atmosphere as hushed and funereal as a tomb, Judge Averill declared the Court in session. He had been preceded by an attendant who carried an armload of books. The judge referred to two of these books, added a note, then looked up. His eyes traveled from Whitley to Farley and rested on Ames.

"After careful consideration of Mr. Ames' petition, it is the decision of this Court that he may be heard. There are, however, reservations. Anything Mr. Ames says here in open court does not provide him immunity to civil action for slander or libel, nor from criminal action proceedings by the State. Mr. Ames may submit documentary evidence but he cannot summon witnesses to testify. Such summons may, however, be ordered by the Court, with or without such application from Mr. Ames, as the Court sees fit.

"Mr. Ames, do you still want to testify?"

"I do, Your Honor."

Both Farley and Whitley quietly entered their "Exception" to the Judge's decision and a few moments later the judge said, "Proceed, Mr. Ames," in a soft voice that carried clearly to every corner of the room.

In complete silence, Ames crossed the well to Sheriff Kaine and took from him a locked, heavy leather bag. He opened the bag and began to empty it of its many papers. Included were official graphs, newspaper clippings, letters, and odd sheets of paper. Ames offered them piece by piece as documentary evidence. As the clerks stamped each piece, Whitley and Farley stood by close at hand. Once or twice there were whispered conferences among them and Ames and Judge Averill. When all the evidence had been entered, Ames stood alone in the center of the well.

"Ladies and gentlemen of the jury, you have heard His Honor declare the bounds within which I must testify. Since I cannot call back many of the witnesses you have heard without the Court's consent, I must first show cause to recall these witnesses. This I intend to do. I intend first, however, to tell you what I know they could and might have told you, had they been properly questioned, and had their testimony been related.

"I intend also to prove that the State's case against Mr. Wylie is a deliberate fraud, entered into knowingly, in secret conspiracy, by the Colonial Attorney and counsel for the defense."

Ames expected the reception this declaration drew from the courtroom and he waited until the storm subsided in a sea of sighs. His eyes roamed the room. He saw Sue Wylie's drawn face beside Tom's study in confidence. He saw the dark, unbelieving, bewildered hope in Buck Wylie's fear-ridden eyes, for Buck knew as well as everyone there that he had been doomed. And he studied the lawyers, the general disbelief and outrage of the staffs, though Whitley looked fierce and stolid and Farley sat in sweating expectancy. He did not look toward Murchison.

"Moreover," Ames resumed, "by documenting the instances in which Mr. Wylie has been left helpless by a combination of circumstance, false testimony, planted evidence and deliberately inadequate defense, I intend also to place before you a clear case indicting the real murderer of Mr. Purdom. To do this I shall have to make statements that will remain hypothetical until the Court, by calling witnesses for me, transforms theory to fact. I ask your patience, please."

HE SAT down carelessly on the edge of his table so that he faced the jury and the courtroom. "First, what is the State's case? They have shown that Purdom, a man of unfailing habit, is missing, and that it is reasonable to assume he is missing because he is dead. They have shown that Wylie and Purdom were secret partners in a claim. They have shown that Purdom met Buck on the 10th, borrowed the *Hellcat* from him for a second time, and then left for an unknown destination with both his ship and Buck's. It is the State's contention that Purdom borrowed the *Hellcat* to bring back a double load of orium, as Buck's partner.

"The State has also, with the services of a perjured witness, Mason, indicated that it may claim that Wylie later followed Purdom in his *Gaucho*. This is refuted by the testimony of Miss Morales alone, who declares he returned that day and stayed home. But the State does not need this line of attack, because it can claim that Wylie knew where Purdom was going anyway. So, using one line or the other, it will claim that Wylie left Mirabello on the 18th, proceeded to where he knew he would find Purdom, and killed him. He then took the *Hellcat* and *Spoon Special* in tow behind his *Gaucho*, came back to Mirabello.

"He landed all three ships in an inconspicuous place, brought the *Gaucho* alone home, then returned, took up the *Hellcat* and *Special* again and went to Grey Mountain. There he planted one of his bombs in the *Special*, set it in a circular course, and returned home with the *Hellcat*, in the expectation that the *Special* would blow up so completely that it would be assumed no trace had been left of Purdom. The murder would be called an accident, cause unknown.

"The motive is self-evident: complete possession of a claim soon to be made public, and presumably very valuable. This value has been indicated by Mr. Murchison not on a basis of fact—for no one seems to have tried to visit this claim—but by pointing out that Purdom was for ten years content to mine his fabulously rich Silver Spoon Mine. It then follows that if he finally did pay attention to another mine, that it must be another bonanza. I do not deny this, and I think it is probably true; the mine must be valuable.

"But it is one thing to establish a motive and another to prove that a man would be willing to kill. I dare say we in this courtroom all have had sufficient motive to contemplate murder at one time or another, without actually murdering. That is because we are not psychologically constituted so as to be able to murder. So the State also had to prove that Wylie is a man so psychologically constituted that he can murder when provided with a powerful motive.

"The point is a very necessary one. Wylie is in his own right an extremely wealthy man. Ordinarily one might question whether a man of such wealth would kill to obtain full ownership of something which was already half his. But the State did not touch upon this vital point at all. Why? Isn't it a remarkable omission? Buck Wylie is a man with a criminal record—"

Farley fairly shouted: "Your Honor, I move for a mistrial!"

Judge Averill paused, then said: "Motion denied."

Ames nodded and went on. "I was about to point out that the State could not bring out Wylie's criminal record without running the risk of a mistrial. But it did not have to think about the problem at all—it was well taken care of for them by Mr. Murchison. The *Twin-Sun* spread the news ably, going so far as to editorialize on Wylie's criminal record. There was no doubt in Mr. Whitley's mind that any jury that might serve in this case would have full knowledge of Wylie's background, including the fact that he was once a gunfighter. And, ladies and gentlemen, if you will search your minds even perfunctorily, you will probably realize how correct Mr. Whitley was.

"But if the job was done for the State by the *Twin-Sun*, why didn't Mr. Farley try to undo it? He knew that Wylie's record was known, that it would mitigate against him. Why didn't he make the effort to show that there was a *reasonable doubt* that a one-time gunfighter, now a wealthy and respectable miner, might not kill for half a claim? That he made no such effort seems to me to be evidence of incompetence or—as I say—of sabotage…"

AMES rubbed his chin reflectively. "But to return. The only proof that Wylie was able to offer *that he was home at noon of the 24th and stayed there* was again Miss Morales. If he was home from noon on, *he could not have been* the man at the helm of the *Hellcat* when it was seen towing the *Special* that afternoon. Miss Morales says so, and if you are to believe her, then you cannot believe the State's case, unless the State produces proof that someone else, at Wylie's behest, did the trick for him. The State has not shown this, since it believes—" and Ames allowed himself to smile, "—that Miss Morales' testimony is worthless."

He got up and paced three feet back and forth, hands behind his back, speaking as he walked. "Skipping lightly over several other facts for the moment—I'll come back to them—let's take a quick look at Wylie's case.

"He was a partner of Purdom's. They filed a mutual claim on February 5th in the Lydonna Group. Probably they had some arrangement for working it—only Wylie's subsequent testimony will establish this. But my guess, based on other things I know, is that Wylie provided the money and machinery—the active management—though Purdom may have been the original discoverer. This would indicate Purdom's trust in Wylie, I think he did trust him, at least in the beginning. Another indication of his trust is a clause in Purdom's partnership agreement with Murchison. I have entered that agreement, seized by Sheriff Kaine, in evidence.

"The agreement has a clause, dated March 2nd, which states that the Purdom-Murchison partnership is confined to the Silver Spoon Mine and has no bearing on any other interest of Purdom's. This means that if Purdom died, Wylie would inherit the other half of their joint claim. We all know how careful and suspicious a man Purdom was. It is hard to believe he would enter into that kind of a partnership with Wylie *unless he trusted him*, since it gave Wylie an obvious interest in Purdom's death." Ames stopped pacing to add, "And I believe that Wylie had full confidence in Purdom.

"He did not question Purdom when he was asked for a loan of the *Hellcat* either the first or the second time. He was, however, careful about it because their partnership was a secret. Open lending of his best ship to Purdom would point suspicion at both of them, so the second time he asked Purdom to go through the motions of fueling the *Hellcat* at Standish, at least in that way making their connection less obvious. I imagine that he was puzzled by Purdom's carelessness that second time, for the first time he lent him the *Hellcat*, it seems both men were very wary.

"And the second time, July 10th, put an extra burden on Wylie because it left him without an available ship. Mason has testified that Wylie ordered him to fuel the *Gaucho* that day. However, from records seized at the Miller Sheds, I can prove that the *Gaucho* was laid up for repairs that day and for some time following—proving Mr. Mason a perjurer of the first order."

HE PAUSED again because of the noise that greeted his last statement, but as soon as he stopped speaking the courtroom grew quiet. At that moment, Farley got up and started out of the courtroom. Two of the sheriff's men unobtrusively accompanied him from the rear of the room.

Ames said: "Here again I pause to ask why the defense made no attempt to gather available documentary proof.

These records were at Miller's Sheds until Sheriff Kaine impounded them, but they were always available. The fact remains...no one asked to see them.

"On July 18th, Wylie left in the *Gaucho* on a prospecting trip. This was a long established custom of his; he always went out the third week of every month, as everyone knew. The State carefully inquired as to Purdom's regular habits, but the defense did not show any interest in Wylie's habits. The defense did, however, employ Mr. Loomis and two men to go to the places Wylie claims he visited on that trip.

"Of course, the State could easily claim that Wylie had killed Purdom at any one of those places or at another, unvisited, place, either near there or en route. The State thus assumes that Wylie knew where his partner, Purdom, was going, and asks you to accept that reasonable assumption. The defense merely lists some six places, pointing out that all were far from the Lydonna claim. It does not attempt to prove, for instance, that Purdom definitely went to the Lydonna claim. It merely hopes you will think so, but perhaps that is because Wylie himself has no idea where Purdom went.

"But let us make our own assumption and let us make it a wild one. Let us assume that Purdom went to none of the six places marked by Wylie, that Wylie met him somewhere else and killed him. If the defense was interested in building up even this poor alibi, why didn't it hire a crack detective to send off on a wild goose chase? First the defense sends a man on a useless errand, and second, it picks a useless man.

"I submit that Mr. Farley knew any testimony offered by Loomis would be worthless, not only because it proved nothing, but because even *if* there was anything to prove, Loomis was *not* the man to do it, as you have seen..."

Ames smiled again and made a little gesture with his hands as he asked the jury: "Who is Loomis? A claim adjuster. Is there anything more futile than sending a paper clerk on a worthless errand? I hardly think so. And you yourselves, ladies and gentlemen, were witnesses to the ease with which the State discredited an eminently discredible witness. Duck soup, from start to finish."

An edge of irony was beginning to form under Ames' words. He had started calmly, speaking in a soft voice and unhurried manner. Now he was sharp, inquisitive, given to gestures. After his last remark he turned to Tisdale with a low bow and murmured, "With no offense to you, Mr. Tisdale. You were brilliant."

Then he clasped his hands and said, "Wylie came back at noon of the 24th. Even Mason does not dispute the time of arrival, but he would if it was necessary. Mason is on somebody's payroll. His testimony still helps the State, because it points out that Wylie was around in time to have left and gotten the *Hellcat* and *Special* if he had left them somewhere. The fact is that Wylie stayed home from that noon until he was arrested the next day by Mr. Whitley— *but can he prove it?*

"Yes," Ames laughed openly, "he can, with the testimony of Miss Morales, *if* you believe her. Can you? Do you?" he demanded. "Look at the way this thing was arranged. Everything questionable happened on a Saturday afternoon, when everyone at the Wylie *arrando* who might be able to testify for him would be sure to be in town. Purdom left the 10th and was due back the 18th—but his ship was not discovered until it coincided with Wylie's return on the 24th. There were people who knew Wylie would leave on or about the 18th—and they knew he would be back on the 24th—*so they held back the discovery of*

Purdom's ship, which they had planted some time before.

"Meanwhile," he held up a hand to stop the noise, "Wylie was left at the mercy of one witness on two occasions—Miss Morales. I submit that had it been deemed necessary, Miss Morales would have testified that Wylie *did* leave on the afternoon of the 24th. That—"

"That's a damn filthy—" Lola Morales screamed, standing up, when Buck Wylie's hand closed on her wrist and yanked her down to her chair. His face was black as a thundercloud. The girl gasped something and started to sob, but Buck muttered something to her that stopped her immediately.

AT THAT moment Farley returned to the courtroom. The deputies left him at the head of the aisle and he went alone to his table. But he did not sit down in the chair he had vacated. He took a seat farthest from Buck and sat with his hands limp in his lap. He looked quite sick.

"I was saying," Ames resumed, "that Miss Morales testified for the defendant, and that she was allowed to do so because the conspirators knew how worthless her testimony was. I submit, and stand ready to prove when Mr. Wylie takes the stand, that Miss Morales has been Mr. Wylie's mistress for some time. But the fact is well known, and though the State did not *prove* it, it did not really require proof more than was offered that Miss Morales was beholden to Wylie, and might be presumed to perjure herself to help him. Thus, she is allowed to give testimony that will not be accepted.

"But even then, you will notice, she did not—and the defense did not really try to build up her case. Mr. Farley left her status as a *friend* clearly open to attack. Had Miss Morales been willing to perjure herself to help Wylie, why did she not, for instance, claim that she was a distant relative—*anything*—rather than let the jury assume what was otherwise almost an open admission that she was prejudiced toward Wylie's favor? Why should a witness who wanted to help Wylie give Mr. Tisdale such contemptuous and meaningless answers? No, she was well chosen for her job, which probably included other minor duties, as I shall presently enumerate.

"And here again," Ames bowed, "Mr. Tisdale shone." He added, more seriously, "I do not mean to impugn Mr. Tisdale, who, I think, is moderately proud of doing an assigned work. That his brilliance resembles paste jewelry is the fault of a paste case. Nor do I say that every witness for the State is guilty of perjury. Not at all.

"Franshaw, Saunders, the Standish traffic managers, the various attendants, all told the truth. They heard the appointment made; they saw the men together. *But they were meant to see and hear!* Mason is a liar, but not entirely. We know he lied about the *Gaucho*, and we may be quite sure he did not overhear Wylie and Purdom discussing their partnership. Both men were much too cautious for that. Mason might have lied about the 24th, however. He might have said that he came to the *arrando* at two o'clock and saw Wylie leaving. That would kill Wylie's story, so why didn't Mason say so?

"Because that would have refuted Miss Morales too directly! It was decided not to build too airtight a case against Wylie. It might begin to smell a little. Leaving him with worthless alibis was good enough and shrewd planning. All this, of course, presupposes a central intelligence, and thus is my central theme.

"Whether Reichard actually saw the *Hellcat* towing the *Special* is for you to decide. Possibly he did, and the conspirators let him live because they were sure he hadn't seen who was at the helm of the *Hellcat*. Possibly then they decided his honest evidence was valuable. Or, he may be a witness along the Mason lines—I cannot say.

"As for Mr. Halliday, no one doubts his story. That he happened along is one of the few genuine accidents in this intrigue, and his brave action serves to throw a penetrating light on the case.

"Halliday prevented the bomb from going off. What if he hadn't prevented it? To be sure, his action preserved a bomb, which is a very damaging bit of evidence against Wylie, on the face of it. But Dr. Ballister has admitted that the bomb could have been traced and its ownership established even if it had been blown to infinitesimal fragments. Had he not admitted it, I could provide six dozen assorted experts who would—"

There was general laughter and Ames himself smiled at his own unconsciously extravagant image. "I submit," he went on, "that the conspirators expected an explosion, and expected to be able to prove, with the help of experts, that the bomb had belonged to Wylie. Halliday left them with the bomb intact, which was just as good or better.

"But look at it from Wylie's point of view. Suppose he actually had wanted to blow up the *Special*, after doing what the State says he did. Wylie has been a miner for some time. He knows bombs and knows they can be traced. Why should he have used one of his own bombs? The State had Dr. Ballister say it would *likely* have been impossible, a statement he later swallowed. But why should Wylie take that chance? Why not get a bomb, somewhere, anywhere—it isn't difficult for a miner— which could *never* be traced to him?"

AMES stroked his face reflectively and said, "No, the plant is too obvious. It fairly shrieks Wylie's innocence. But it does more than that. It asks two important questions.

"First, what happened to Purdom's body? If Purdom was murdered, why not put his body in the *Special* and have the investigation assume he was killed in the explosion? Had there been an explosion we might never have known whether or not Purdom or his body was in the ship. Now we know Purdom wasn't in it.

"Second, what about the bomb itself? The Wylie *arrando* employs many people. How many of these people had access to the underground bomb shed? I do not pretend to know, but I do know that *at least one person* besides Wylie had access to it, because Wylie didn't take that bomb—so who did? Possibly Mason? Possibly Miss Morales helped him? She has complete run of the place. At any rate, this line of questioning was never attempted by the defense, elementary though it appears. Why?

"Why?" Ames asked again. "When I first became interested in the case professionally, I was struck by the number of times I had to ask myself why. The question of Purdom's body convinced me that something was wrong, and various other circumstances increased that conviction. I was running down some of my suspicions when I was fired by Wylie, but since I knew who was behind that advised action, I realized I was proceeding correctly. As a material witness—"

He paused, grinning. "At this point I should like to insert, purely for the record, that I was drunk because I had to be; it was my one chance to re-enter the case with some authority, and it enabled me to get the records, documents, etc. that I needed." He paused again and studied first

Whitley, then Farley. He did look toward Murchison; he had once glanced at him. His grin was gone when he spoke again.

"I think I have indicated sufficiently the lines along which Wylie's innocence can be proven. They seem to me much better than the defense's obvious intention to cling to the assertion that Purdom is not dead, but has disappeared—a curious defense in the face of so many curious incriminating facts. But the best proof of Wylie's innocence is proof of another's guilt. From here on my testimony is concerned with lodging the guilt where it belongs.

"If I am correct in what I have said so far, it is apparent that Wylie is the victim of a concerted plot, and that the plotters are people who knew his habits, his business, his background. I submit, and will prove, that these plotters include at least Mr. John Murchison, Miss Lola Morales, one Jake Webber, not present, and to some extent, the Colonial Attorney, Mr. Whitley and counsel for the defense, Mr. Farley..."

AGAIN it was necessary to halt the trial while Judge Averill gave final warning that the next outbreak would be the last before the courtroom was cleared. Ames scarcely paid any attention to the vast outpouring of shouts, screams, cries, applause, moans, sobs and sighs. He measured off his three feet of floor and paced them, and when it was quiet again, some minutes later, he spoke.

"Such a conspiracy could only be fathered by the possibility of great profit to all involved. I submit that such profit did, and does today exist, and that the stakes of the game were not only the Silver Spoon Mine, but all of Wylie's vast holdings to the last red cent, and also the new claim in which Wylie and Purdom were partners.

"On February 5th, Wylie and Purdom became partners. Murchison knew something of the sort had happened by March 2nd, for on that day Purdom entered the limiting clause in his partnership agreement with Murchison. Until that time Purdom had had no other interests but the Silver Spoon—so the moment he confined his Murchison partnership to the Silver Spoon, Murchison knew other interests had come into existence.

"It took him six days to find out, by one means or another, that Wylie was involved, for on March 8th, Murchison graphed the I. P. Regional Headquarters and made inquiries on Wylie's criminal record. He had known about it before; now he wanted the complete info. On March 11th the I. P. furnished the info, and Murchison carefully filed it away for future reference. He subsequently used it the day Wylie was arrested, and thus performed a public service—after keeping it more than four months! But he also used it in another way. I'll come to that soon.

"On April 15th Murchison became the possessor of information that provided additional power to his motive. Before that he had already deemed to operate on Wylie, but April 15th clinched it. For on that day the Interplanetary Colonial Council passed an amendment to the Criminal Code which applied to the colonies here, and which suited him perfectly. That amendment was Section—ah—Section 4551.

"That amendment stated that in the event of a criminal act, any person injured by that act, even indirectly, could not only sue for damages, but could claim a penalty judgment against the criminal's entire possessions. For instance, a man is killed by a pirate, and the man's wife is his legal heiress. Under the new Section the wife's claim does not end with the State's—which is to exact the penalty for murder—but also gives her legal claim to everything the pirate owned. That claim is a penalty judgment, and supersedes all other claims, those of the State included.

"It applied to Murchison as well. He and Purdom were mutually each other's heir in their partnership. If Purdom were murdered—say, by Wylie, then Murchison would not only inherit the Silver Spoon *but he could claim and get everything Wylie owned!* What could be sweeter? He had been thinking of killing Purdom and framing Wylie before, but now he began to act. The first thing he did was to violate the ordinance that compelled the *Twin-Sun* to publish the new law. He didn't publish it. It was hardly worth hiding—who would have paid much attention to it? —but he was covering every trail from then on.

"Two obstacles lay in his way, however. The first was that he didn't know where the Silver Spoon Mine was. He might inherit it, but it would remain an inheritance on paper, Probably he had many times thought over ways and means of doing away with Purdom, but he hadn't hit on a way that would also reveal the mine's location. That thought must have occurred to Purdom too, for he guarded his secret as if his life depended on it, which it did. As long as Murchison didn't know where the mine was, he had an interest in keeping Purdom alive, and he drew his share of the enormous profits.

"The second obstacle was finding a way to frame Wylie. As it subsequently turned out, the answer to one led to the answer of the second. He devised an extremely clever way of doing both…"

AMES let his voice down and for the first time he faced Murchison directly. Not a sound came from the rapt audience. Murchison returned his gaze tolerantly and then a slow, pleasant smile broke on his face. "Please go on," he said. He folded his arms across his chest.

Ames nodded complaisantly.

"Murchison began to work on Purdom. Through hints and sly insinuations he began building up Purdom's latest mistrust of everyone until it included the one man, Wylie, he had trusted. And then he focused his attention on Wylie, convincing Purdom that he had ways of knowing that Wylie was shadowing him, or attempting to. Murchison pretended to be concerned only with protecting the Silver Spoon. Purdom didn't know that Murchison knew about his partnership with Wylie, so when he received repeated warnings about Wylie, it meant only one thing to him—that Wylie was using their partnership to get at the Silver Spoon. By June he had Purdom jittery, and then he suggested ways and means of keeping Wylie off his trail.

"By then too, of course, he had arranged his alliance with Mr. Whitley and Miss Morales. They were ready to play their parts.

"Sometime early in June, before Purdom left on one of his trips to the Silver Spoon, he asked Wylie to lend him the *Hellcat* to take with him. He did this to make sure that Wylie wouldn't follow him, because the only other ship Wylie owned that was fast enough to keep the *Special* in sight was the *Gaucho*, and she was in the Miller Sheds for one of her numerous overhaulings. If he had the *Hellcat*, he could be reasonably sure that Wylie couldn't follow him to the *Silver Spoon*.

"He told Wylie he wanted it because he was expecting a

storm in his mining area and wanted to pull a double load before the storm broke. Wylie probably didn't believe him but asked no questions. Purdom had never used this common custom before, but he also had not had a partner before, and maybe he was taking advantage of the partnership by getting free use of a ship. It didn't bother Wylie except that it meant they had to do the whole thing secretly.

"But now Murchison knew that Purdom was going to the Silver Spoon with two vessels. That gave him his chance. He knew Purdom's habits and got around them. He knew that whenever Purdom returned from a trip to the Silver Spoon the first thing he did was to take the *Special* to Miller and have the Berry gauge moved back to zero. Miller had to take his glasses off before Purdom would allow him to get near the gauge—to illustrate Purdom's extreme caution. Because of this, and because he knew too well how miserly Purdom was, Murchison correctly assumed that Purdom wasted no fuel going to and from the *Silver Spoon*, and that if he could get at the figures on the gauge, that they would reveal almost to a certainty where the *Silver Spoon* was—a fact he had to know.

"He couldn't get at the *Special's* gauge, but he had worked out a way to get at the *Hellcat's*. And since he knew both ships were going to the same place that time, one was as good as the other. So, on June 12th Murchison went to Miller and asked him to get the figures on the Hellcat's gauge. His pretext was an investigation for the *Twin-Sun* on something concerning Wylie, and to back it up he showed Miller the criminal record he had received from the I. P. months before.

"The *Hellcat* wasn't in the sheds then and Miller wasn't

expecting her—actually she was out with Purdom, and Murchison expected her back soon—but Miller refused out of loyalty to Wylie. The next day, June 13th, according to a copy seized by Sheriff Kaine, Murchison came back and presented Miller with an authorization to surrender the data. It was signed by the Colonial Attorney, Mr. Whitley. But the *Hellcat* wasn't there—not yet. It came in, according to Miller's records, on June 16th, brought in by Wylie himself. And Purdom arrived at the same time with the *Special*.

"What had happened was that Purdom brought the *Hellcat* back to Wylie, who then immediately took it to Miller, with Purdom right behind him. When they arrived together, to Miller it appeared to be nothing more than a coincidence—he had no way of knowing that both ships had been to the same place and had just returned. He was surprised that Wylie also wanted his Berry gauge zeroed, but he did it. While Purdom's main concern was keeping Wylie busy, he kept an eye on Miller to make sure that Miller was working on the *Special* without his glasses.

"But then his vigilance relaxed a little. When Miller went to the *Hellcat's* gauge, he copied down the readings he found there. After both men left, Miller called Murchison in obedience to the C.A.'s authorization and turned over the readings to him.

"And that told Murchison where the Silver Spoon was."

AMES stopped, blew his breath out noisily and returned to sit on an edge of his table. He seemed wearied by the length of his address to the jury, but the knowledge that he was nearing the climax gave him new energy. He wondered how close to the end Murchison's calm would last.

"I said," he resumed, "that Murchison found out where the Silver Spoon was. The task might have been difficult, but the fact is that the mine was so located that a Berry gauge reading was a dead giveaway. I will presently go into this in some detail, but in part it explains Purdom's concern for the gauge.

"After Murchison's exploratory trip to the Silver Spoon, taken with his chauffeur, Jake Webber, he waited for his chance. He let Purdom make another trip in the latter part of June, unmolested, because Wylie was off prospecting and Purdom had gone in his *Special* alone. On the 10th of July, however, he asked Wylie for the *Hellcat* again. Possibly he meant that to be the last time, since by today, August 5th, their partnership would be made public.

"Again Wylie consented, but notice how Purdom went about making himself safe. He called Wylie from the Racketeer's Cafe and used the phone *at the bar!* He made an appointment at Standish port and twice that day was seen with Wylie. He was plainly hoping that any hostile notions Wylie might have been nursing would be deterred by such publicity. At any rate, after fuelling his ship at Standish, he and Wylie left together. Some fifty miles out they space-anchored. Purdom took Wylie back to the *arrando* in his own ship, returned to the *Hellcat*, took her in tow and went on to the Silver Spoon.

"Coincidentally enough," Ames cocked his brows, "Murchison left Mirabello on July 16th to attend a newspaper convention at Church's. Had there not been a convention, Murchison would have found another excuse to be away. He attended that convention, all right, and the Twin-Sun ran a photo of him there on the 19th.

"The *Twin-Sun's* society notes did not, however, mention the fact that on the way to Church's, Murchison and Webber stopped at the Silver Spoon and murdered Purdom before they continued their merry trip.

"The convention ended on the 21st. Murchison's ship was fast enough to have made that trip in forty hours. But it took him three days to go there and three to come back, so that he returned, according to his own admission, on the evening of the fateful 24th. Why? Because when he left Church's he came back to the Silver Spoon to bring back the *Hellcat* and the *Special!*

"He had one poor stroke of luck, though. He had meant to bring back Purdom's body and have it blown up in the *Special's* explosion. But he had killed Purdom in one of the mineshafts, and Purdom had been effectively buried under an enormous orium deposit. He couldn't get Purdom out quickly, so he had to leave him in the mine.

"The rest worked out on schedule. He already had one of Wylie's demolition bombs, supplied by Mason or Miss Morales, and it was planted in the *Special.* Murchison and Webber waited somewhere off Mirabello with the *Hellcat* and *Special* in tow, and when Wylie returned at noon of the 24th, Miss Morales signaled the tidings from an AV transmitter in the living room of Wylie's own home. Webber got into the *Hellcat* and towed in the *Special.* If Reichard told the truth, that was what he saw. No wonder the *Hellcat* wouldn't return his signals, if he signaled. Over Grey Mountain, Webber went aboard the *Special,* put her into a slow circle, lit the fuse and got out.

"He knew there was no one at the Wylie *arrando* on a Saturday afternoon, so he brought the *Hellcat* in to the Wylie blastport. Then he made his way back to town unseen. Some hours later, Murchison, alone in his ship, elected to come home. It was a quiet return, and no one seems to have noticed whether or not Webber was with him. The Twin-Sun, so eager to report Murchison's departure and arrival at Church's, did not see fit to mention his return.

"The next morning Murchison composed his editorial denouncing Wylie and exposing his criminal record."

THE stillness of the courtroom was faintly oppressive now. It measured and emphasized Ames' occasional pauses for breath. Murchison no longer smiled, but there was no suspicion of trouble on his face. He seemed deeply interested and attentive, nothing more.

Now Ames took out several sheets of paper from among those submitted in evidence. "These," he explained, "are copies of the readings from the Berry gauges of the *Hellcat*, the *Spoon Special* and the *Gaucho*. They have been certified and the unsealing process photographed. I am aware of the fact that such readings are apt to be worthless, but in this instance, as I will prove, they actually proved to be the key..."

He went on for some ten minutes, explaining the notations, dwelling in particular upon the point 3 reading, and gradually, without emphasizing the point, he slipped into an account of his voyage to the Silver Spoon within the Hive. He recounted the almost incredible details, the appearance of the crazy asteroid, the mine itself, Webber's appearance and the duel in the hills. He ended by mentioning the explosion of Murchison's ship and Webber's confession.

"The confession," he admitted, "is unfortunately not much good because Webber was too far gone when he signed it. But every statement I have made is substantiated by one or another of the facts I have submitted in evidence. Together they make up a case that is, considering the circumstances, amazing clear, and they point to John Murchison as the man responsible for the murder of Scotty Purdom..."

In the silence, Judge Averill said, "Mr. Ames, do you wish to call any witnesses or to cross-question any previously offered testimony?"

"If it please the Court, I should like to question Mr. Murchison."

"Mr. John Murchison will take the stand."

Murchison rose unhurriedly, walked down the aisle into the well and stood before the bench. "Your Honor," he said quietly, "I have nothing to hide under ordinary circumstances. I would welcome—I would insist on—being allowed the privilege of answering the fantastic charges made by Mr. Ames. However, I am so stunned and so...so completely shocked by these cunning and malicious perversions of the truth that I cannot, in fairness to myself, take the stand at this time. I state my innocence unequivocally and completely, but it nevertheless behooves me to stand on my constitutional rights, and to refuse to testify on the grounds that my testimony may tend to incriminate and degrade me."

Judge Averill was silent for a moment. He studied Murchison in a strangely preoccupied way, then sighed and said, "Mr. Murchison, you are not on trial here, and you do not have the rights of the accused in refusing the stand. Moreover, you have already, of your own free will, testified in this court. As a witness, your testimony is open to cross-examination. This Court has granted Mr. Ames the right of summoning witnesses, and it orders you to take the stand."

Murchison hesitated. "And if I refuse, Your Honor?"

"You will be held in contempt of court," the Judge

answered gravely. "And I will immediately summon the grand jury to undertake indictment proceedings against you. Surely such a course is ill-advised for an innocent man?"

Again Murchison hesitated. Presently he shrugged and walked to the witness box. He faced Ames calmly enough, but with an expression that was at once patient and suggestive of restrained fury. It was as if he were saying, "I'll do what I must, now, but I will straighten our account in the future for this hopeless and baseless inquisition." But all he said was, "Yes, Mr. Ames?"

Ames said, "Do you deny Webber's story—that you stopped him from trying to kill me after that day he took a shot at me—that you—"

"I'll make it easier for you, Mr. Ames. I deny everything. I deny every last word that tries to implicate me in any way."

Ames nodded but asked: "You deny ever having been on the asteroid where the Silver Spoon Mine is?"

"Suppose I ask you, Mr. Ames, to produce the slightest shred of evidence that I ever was there—if indeed you do know where it is—instead of building up your fantastic case by repeating false allegations. What proof have you aside from a supposed confession which you yourself have declared worthless?"

"You haven't answered my question."

"That I deny having been to the secret Silver Spoon? Of course I deny it."

"Because if you admitted it, you would be admitting that my fantastic case was not without basis?"

"Rather," said Murchison, "because if you prove it, you will prove your case. And unless you do offer proof instead of involved speeches, I am afraid I can't help you, my insane young friend."

Ames nodded again. "I agree with you, Mr. Murchison. If you'll bear with me, I will furnish the jury with the proof—or, at least, with what I consider the beginning of irrefutable proof. Keep your seat, Mr. Murchison, I won't be long."

Ames turned to the jury. "I did not mention, in my summation, that Tom Blake and I brought back the body of the late Jake Webber. In addition, we brought back Purdom's dog, Duke. We did this because of a curious physical phenomenon that seems to be endemic on the asteroid where the Silver Spoon is. Rather than contenting myself with describing it, I will demonstrate it and let you judge for yourselves."

AFTER a brief consultation with Sheriff Kaine, attendants brought in a large screen, oval-shaped and mounted on a stand that brought it to a height of seven feet, and a white cabinet. When the cabinet was opened, it revealed an inner board studded with dials and switches, and from which a conic projector, somewhat like a small searchlight, was brought out. A man, identified as a laboratory expert attached to Kaine's staff, came forward in a white coat. He flicked on a switch and a scarcely visible beam of light played on the screen. He twiddled dials until the light vanished altogether.

"This cabinet," Ames explained, "houses a miniature radium detector. By utilizing an invisible light wavelength it picks up traces of a rare radium-like substance. Dr. Lowell here will explain it more fully later. It has, however, an immediate application."

Ames then called Tom Blake. Sour Tom made his way into the well with his usual acid expression. Ames asked him to stand behind the screen, which was backed by a window on which the shades had been drawn. Tom walked behind the screen. Only his legs showed under it. Dr. Lowell fussed with the dials again. Slowly, a light appeared behind the screen. It grew brighter and took form. Within fifteen seconds it had outlined in light the mass of Tom's head and both his hands.

"Leave the cabinet now, please, Doctor," Ames instructed. To the jury he then said, "It appears that the asteroid on which the Silver Spoon is located is one of those System rarities which contains in its atmosphere a huge mass of these suspended radium-like particles; Anyone setting foot on that asteroid, even for a moment, would pick up enough of those particles on his exposed skin to show up easily on this screen. This effect lasts no longer than a month at most. In other words, such a result—this bright outline—could not be gotten from anyone who had not been on that asteroid within the past month.

"The nearest known System body that might produce this result is in the Mercurian Innesta Group, and in that case the particles could be subjected to laboratory tests, since they differ."

He then asked Tom to sit down again and Dr. Lowell himself went behind the screen. Nothing happened; he remained hidden. After him the Sheriff and two more men went behind the screen with the same negative results. Then Ames regarded Murchison.

Murchison was sitting with his hands folded across his chest, a supercilious, saddened smile on his face.

Ames said nothing and walked behind the screen. Those on the other side could see his head and hands appear. Then they watched his hands open his collar and part of his neck appeared. A minute later he came out, buttoning his shirt.

To the jury he said: "I think my point is apparent now. I have had the body of Jake Webber subjected to this test. Dr. Lowell has also tested the body of Purdom's dog. When Purdom's body is brought back, the same tests can be applied." He turned to Murchison and walked to him. "Mr. Murchison, will you be so good as to step behind that screen?"

Murchison made no answer. His eyes seemed half closed but he did not move. His smile persisted and he said nothing. His attitude, with his folded arms, seemed faintly defiant.

"Well, Mr. Murchison?" Ames asked.

When Murchison still made no move, Judge Averill said quite sharply: "Need I remind you, Mr. Murchison, that your—"

He did not finish what he was saying, for suddenly Sheriff Kaine came forward swiftly. He walked directly to Murchison and touched his arm. The touch was enough to unbalance the sitting body. For it was no more than a body. As it sprawled forward into the sheriff's arms, its folded arms came apart, and as the right hand fell, a small-barreled Foster gun rolled out of the relaxed grip and clattered to the floor. Only then did they see the shoulder holster that had held it concealed. Below the holster a small hole had burned through Murchison's heart. The heat ray had passed through his body and touched the chair, and it was the tiny wisp of smoke behind the chair that Kaine had seen.

Murchison had held on to the end...

IT WAS some four days before the wearied reporters

finally found Ames, an accomplishment made possible only by their shrewd, desperate bribe to a small boy named Willy, who said he thought Ames was fishing, and who said he thought he knew where. And laden with enough candy to open his own shop, Willy led them through tall grass to the edge of a stream where Ames was, indeed, fishing.

Beside him sat Tom, and a little further off, unpacking a picnic basket, was Sue Wylie. Ames spoke to the reporters only because, as he told them, he was in a hurry to get on with the picnic. He parried all questions about the disposition of Whitley, Farley, Lola Morales and the others on the grounds that he was to be called as a witness against them, and consequently could not discuss the case.

"Hah!" one bitter reporter laughed. "Now you're extra-legal again, eh? What about commenting on that story Sheriff Kaine out—the one about that test being a fake?"

"A fake?" Ames inquired mildly. "It did the job, I thought."

"Yeah, but you and this fellow Tom Blake rubbed a kind of ointment on your face and hands, didn't you? You got that stuff in a jar in a drugstore in town, didn't you?"

"Mmmmm," was Ames' nodded agreement.

"Well?" fifteen voices demanded, pencils poised.

Ames scratched his head. "If you gentlemen will look through the testimony I gave, you may notice that I did not specify that either Webber's body, or the dog's—or, for that matter, Purdom's, or even Murchison's, would react the same way. I merely said the tests had been applied to the dog and Webber. I did not say whether the results were the same. As a matter of fact, they weren't. There's a law against tampering with evidence, you know."

"What about you and Blake being evidence? What about that?"

Ames nodded. "I don't pretend I didn't know what I was doing," he said. "Tom and I were free to use any ointment we wanted, and to use any kind of screen—the screen was an ordinary linen and there was no light, you might care to know. But had Murchison dared, he could have brazened it out, and cross-examination, or questioning of Dr. Lowell, would have brought out the truth. I just didn't think Murchison would go behind the screen."

"But what if he had?"

"No," Ames said, and shook his head. "You see—" He broke off and began playing his line carefully. A moment later he yanked out a small, lustrous blue fish. It landed struggling on the grass, and then began to change color. It turned dead white, then pink, then redder and redder, and all the while it was blowing itself up until it was several times its previous size. Suddenly it exploded and only its lips were left. The astonished gallery watched Ames use the lips for bait and he cast out easily and relaxed.

"That was a crazy-baiter," Ames observed. "Astonished you, but not me. Reason: I'm an experienced fisherman. It's the same in law and in life. You have to know what you're fishing for. You see, there are some fish that just won't be caught. If you catch them, they either break away and confess, or they explode...or they kill themselves..." He sighed. "I didn't expect anything as dramatic as a courtroom suicide, but I knew my fish. I knew he wouldn't step behind the screen. And when I yanked him out there for everyone to have a look...he exploded, that's all..."

"And," said Sue Wylie, coming up, "if you people don't leave Ames to his lunch now, there'll be another explosion in about a minute."

"You, dear?" Ames asked.

"Me, dear," Sue said.

"Then there'd be nothing left but your beautiful lips."

"Yes, dear."

Sour Tom got up with a groan, "This, folks," he announced acidly, "goes on all day. Any wonder them darn fish get apoplexy?"

He had to run to catch up to the quickly retreating newspapermen.

THE END

If you've enjoyed this book, you will not want to miss these terrific titles…

ARMCHAIR SCI-FI, FANTASY, & HORROR DOUBLE NOVELS, $12.95 each

D-1 **THE GALAXY RAIDERS** by William P. McGivern
SPACE STATION #1 by Frank Belknap Long

D-2 **THE PROGRAMMED PEOPLE** by Jack Sharkey
SLAVES OF THE CRYSTAL BRAIN by William Carter Sawtelle

D-3 **YOU'RE ALL ALONE** by Fritz Leiber
THE LIQUID MAN by Bernard C. Gilford

D-4 **CITADEL OF THE STAR LORDS** by Edmund Hamilton
VOYAGE TO ETERNITY by Milton Lesser

D-5 **IRON MEN OF VENUS** by Don Wilcox
THE MAN WITH ABSOLUTE MOTION by Noel Loomis

D-6 **WHO SOWS THE WIND...** by Rog Phillips
THE PUZZLE PLANET by Robert A. W. Lowndes

D-7 **PLANET OF DREAD** by Murray Leinster
TWICE UPON A TIME by Charles L. Fontenay

D-8 **THE TERROR OUT OF SPACE** by Dwight V. Swain
QUEST OF THE GOLDEN APE by Ivar Jorgensen and Adam Chase

D-9 **SECRET OF MARRACOTT DEEP** by Henry Slesar
PAWN OF THE BLACK FLEET by Mark Clifton.

D-10 **BEYOND THE RINGS OF SATURN** by Robert Moore Williams
A MAN OBSESSED by Alan E. Nourse

ARMCHAIR SCIENCE FICTION CLASSICS, $12.95 each

C-1 **THE GREEN MAN**
by Harold M. Sherman

C-2 **A TRACE OF MEMORY**
By Keith Laumer

ARMCHAIR MASTERS OF SCIENCE FICTION SERIES, $16.95 each

M-1 **MASTERS OF SCIENCE FICTION, Vol. One**
Bryce Walton—"Dark of the Moon" and other tales

M-2 **MASTERS OF SCIENCE FICTION, Vol. Two**
Jerome Bixby: "One Way Street" and other tales

If you've enjoyed this book, you will not want to miss these terrific titles…

ARMCHAIR SCI-FI & HORROR DOUBLE NOVELS, $12.95 each

www.ingramcontent.com/pod-product-compliance
Lightning Source LLC
Chambersburg PA
CBHW030326180626
46810CB00003B/1240